TAILWIND TALES

Uplifting Real Life Stories

LALITA ANAND

Brought To You By Teenage Foundation

notionpress.com

INDIA · SINGAPORE · MALAYSIA

CONTENTS

Foreword 7

Acknowledgements 9

01   Awe Inspiring 11

02   The Right Time 17

03   First Crush 23

04   Mother's Mother 33

05   Adrenaline Rush...But Safety First 49

06   The Girl on the Bicycle 57

07   Give Back to Nature 65

08   Konda and Kutty 75

09   Myra's Odyssey 85

10   Echoes of a Lost Son 99

11   Drug Bust 107

12   Bougainvillea Blooms 115

13   From Rush Hour to Solitude 119

FOREWORD

I am Dr. Lalita Anand, a teacher and mother of two young men who were once adolescents . Over my 30 years of teaching and research, I have interacted with countless students, from 10-year-olds in class V to those at ISB with an average age of 27. I have witnessed their struggles and have been fortunate enough to help them find solutions.

It has always concerned me to see teenagers burdened by expectations from their parents while grappling with their own desires. I often wondered, "Don't these teenagers have dreams of their own? Wouldn't they want something for themselves too? Have we ever paused to ask them?" These questions deeply resonated with me and fuelled my search for answers.

In my observations, I noticed that teenagers faced various challenges: mismatches between their abilities and choices, the influence of peer pressure, excessive immersion in computers and mobiles due to loneliness and lack of direction, battles with insecurities, low self-confidence, and alternating phases of depression and aggression. Sometimes, these struggles led to tragic outcomes due to risky actions. Unfortunately, these issues often went unnoticed and unspoken, leaving many of us unaware of their silent battles.

The rising rates of juvenile crime and the increasing number of teenage suicides deeply affected me. I realised there was a gap between how we should be supporting teenagers and how we actually are. Today's seeds are tomorrow's trees, and these young minds will shape the future. This realisation made me question whether they are truly prepared to face the world and if they have the resources needed to navigate societal challenges. Who will walk with them on this journey?

As my own children grew, so did my understanding. Conversations with my father offered valuable insights, guiding me to transform my thoughts into action. This journey culminated in the creation of the Teenage Foundation, an NGO dedicated to supporting young people.

For the longest time, I wanted to write a book to inspire teenagers. Just as a tailwind helps an airplane soar, "Tailwind Tales" is designed to motivate every teenager who reads it.

To all the wonderful children and remarkable teenagers out there, I wish you all the very best.

ACKNOWLEDGEMENTS

Firstly, I would like to express my deepest gratitude to my late father, Shri R. Subramanyam, who had authored a couple of books himself, and my mother, Smt. Valli Subramanyam, who is a Gazal Singer. Their unwavering encouragement and belief in my abilities have always inspired me to write and pursue my other interests, such as Classical Dance and Music.

I am deeply thankful to my dear husband, C.V. Anand, whose support has been immeasurable. His patience in reading through numerous drafts and providing insightful suggestions has been invaluable.

This acknowledgment would be incomplete without me mentioning my children. I extend my heartfelt thanks to my sons, Milind, Nikhil, and daughter-in-law, Aishwarya, for inspiring and supporting me as I wrote this book.

I am grateful to Mr. Ravi Subramanyan, who has been a guiding force for the Teenage Foundation since its very beginning. His thoughtful feedback on my drafts and his creative suggestion for the book's title have been truly indispensable.

A special thanks to Ms. Ranjana Sharma for her meticulous editing and valuable suggestions, which significantly enhanced my work.

Last but not the least, my sincere thanks to D. V. Krishna Chaitanya for his assistance with formatting, styling, and collating my work.

01

AWE INSPIRING

Motivating others is a leader's quality!

It was the year 2000. My husband, Mr. C V Anand, an IPS officer of the 1991 batch of the then united Andhra Pradesh cadre, got transferred from the post of Superintendent of Police, Krishna District, to Deputy Commissioner of Police, East Zone, Hyderabad. Shifting and settling down from a district to a city was exciting indeed! Since I was born in Hyderabad and had spent most of my growing years here, it all happened seamlessly.

I became a member of an association called the IPS Officers' Wives Association (IPSOWA). The officers' wives would meet once a month over lunch or high tea. The organisation helped strengthen the bond of the police fraternity and also conducted some welfare activities for the families in the force. There was always warmth and a sense of belonging here.

It is here that I first met Smt. Vimala, wife of retired IPS officer Mr. S. Anandram and niece of the late author R.K. Narayan and cartoonist R.K. Laxman. Fair-complexioned and delicately built, she had long hair securely braided. Draped in a simple cotton sari, her countenance was minimalistic and understated. I was charmed by her elegance as I watched her socialising with all the junior officers' wives. One day, after our lunch, the members sat down to discuss the "Family-Night", an evening of bonding, fun, and entertainment for the officers and their families, an annual event organised by IPSOWA.

As the committee members brainstormed on what to do, Vimala ma'am spoke, "May I suggest a tableau? It's titled **Women of India**. I have penned the script." Everyone got interested and listened to her with rapt attention as she explained the concept. "On stage, the focus light will converge on a spot where participants dressed as famous women of India will appear one by one. In the background, their details will be read out by one of you. Put in some music, and a wonderful tableau is in place."

Everyone clapped their hands on hearing this. There was huge enthusiasm and participation by the ladies. Excitement was tangible as rehearsals, and subsequently, costume rehearsals ensued. The D-Day arrived, and the programme was a grand success. My admiration for her grew. I realised she was such a positive force, always inspiring, always motivating people around.

We would often meet at lunches and formal occasions. She would always make it a point to chat with me and find out about my family and other pursuits. In 2006, I had started writing fiction. 'It's a love story,' I disclosed to her. She was very excited to hear this. "Even I have been writing short stories," she revealed. One day, I went to ma'am's house for tea. She handed me a few handwritten papers and asked me to read them and give her an honest opinion. I took them home and read them. True to her lineage, she wrote proficiently. The short story I read was about a policeman and his dedication to duty, the sacrifices he made in life. It was a moving tale.

Next time I met her, I gave her a very positive report about her writing. She asked me to share my writing as well. I was too shy and lacked self-confidence to share it with her, so I bargained for time and said, "Will surely do so at a later date."

Life marched on. I started working as a Teaching Assistant and then as a Researcher at ISB. Later on, I did a PhD in Finance from IIT Madras, which took almost 6 years of my life. I stopped going to IPSOWA meetings.

I got very busy with my own life, kids, work, and so many other things that I lost touch with ma'am. Many years later, when I went to the ladies' lunch, I could not find ma'am. I found out that she had grown old and far too frail to commute and come to the Police Mess for socialising. She continued to be in my thoughts.

One day, I received a phone call from her. She asked me to visit her. I was delighted at the prospect of meeting her. I made her favourite dish, the Avial[1], and took it along. I met Sir there too. She received me with warmth and love. After exchanging pleasantries, she enquired once again about my writings, and I about hers. She showed me a bundle of handwritten papers and said she had completed them. "Now they remain to be published," she said. She also praised me and my talents, and she always inspired me to complete my book and publish it.

A couple of years later, I developed a slipped disc and was bedridden for a while. My condition worsened, and I could not even sit or walk. Doctors advised surgery. Spine surgery was a major risk, but I had no option. After the operation, I had severe cramps and spasms in my legs. I was bedridden and recovering when I got a call from ma'am. She said her book 'Mangalapuram Tales' was published and was going to be released by Shri E.S.L. Narasimhan, Honourable

---

1   *Avial is mixed vegetables cooked in coconut milk - a delicacy popular in Kerala.*

Governor of Telangana and Andhra Pradesh States. She invited me to the event. I congratulated her and expressed happiness over this wonderful development. I expressed my inability to come due to health issues.

She felt sad for my condition and expressed concern and offered to visit me. I totally refused. ma'am was close to 88 years now, and Anandram Sir was probably ninety-three. Both had become so frail and delicate that they couldn't move out of their house. Governor Narsimhan, who was a former IPS[2] officer himself, knew Sir and ma'am very well. He had first met them at NPA[3] 50 years ago when he was an under trainee and later when he was ASP[4] Nandyal, he had worked under Sir who was then the DIG[5] at Kurnool. He had offered to release the book at their residence itself to avoid exertion to ma'am and Sir. The event went off very well and was covered in all leading newspapers and media.

A few months later, I slowly started moving around and feeling better. Ma'am called me once again and insisted that she wanted to come home to see me. I tried to discourage her, thinking it would tire her, but she was adamant.

At 4 pm, she arrived at my door punctually. I was overjoyed to see her.

Every minute, I felt bad that I had troubled her. She gave me a signed copy of the book she had authored and said, "Now it's time for you to finish your book and publish it." I had long ago given up on that project. She asked me to read out a few lines from my writings. Happy to share, I fetched my book and read it out for her. "You write so well. I want you to complete this book. Meet me every month and give me a report on its progress. I want to see you done with it."

---

2   *IPS – Indian Police Service*
3   *NPA- National Police Academy*
4   *ASP- Assistant Superintendent of Police*
5   *DIG – Deputy Inspector General of Police*

Tears welled in my eyes as I helped her stand when she got ready to leave. Slowly, she descended the steps and sat in her car. She waved to me as the car moved past me. Had God sent her to give me direction and motivation to complete my work? She was awe-inspiring, I thought, as a warm feeling spread across my heart.

Author's Speak

In passion projects such as writing, painting, singing, and dancing, a lot of discipline has to be put in. When motivation, such as that provided by Vimala ma'am, comes our way, it's a cherry on top of the cake!

02

THE RIGHT TIME

There is a right time for everything in life!

It was the summer of 2009. I had turned 40 years of age. Both my sons had grown up and required less of my attention. Anand, my husband who served in the Indian Police Service, had completed his tenure in the districts and was posted in the city. I thought it was the best time to pursue my dream of higher studies. After passing my entrance exam and clearing the interview, I got shortlisted for the Doctoral Programme in Finance at IIT[6] Madras. In fact, I was the first to utilise the tie-up between ISB[7] and IITM on Research while serving as a Teaching Assistant in ISB.

I was overjoyed. It was an honour to be a student once again, that too at the Indian Institute of Technology Madras, one of the oldest and most prestigious academic institutions in the country.

The university campus was very beautiful. Old banyan trees with long cluster roots reaching the ground, deer, and black bucks running

6   *Indian Institute of Technology*
7   *Indian School of Business*

around, making it an exotic place. I was so fascinated by this mini-city. Spread over 250 acres, it had so many departments and centres of excellence, hostels, stores, food courts, staff quarters, and so on. Room 238, Sarayu Hostel, became my address for the next few months while I did my coursework. DOMS, short for Department of Management Studies, located near Gajendra Circle, became my alma mater.

On the first day at DOMS, I met Kartika Nair, a research scholar in finance. I was impressed by how tall and elegant she was. Her thick, black, curly tresses occupied the pride of place on her shoulders. She wore a salwar suit with the dupatta neatly pinned on both sides of her shoulders. A tiny line of sandalwood paste over the bindi on her forehead, a gold chain around her neck, and earrings gave her a traditional look. Her perfect English had a mild Malayali ring to it. Her beautiful eyes, charming smile, and lovely voice made me take to her instantly. We hit it off at once. I asked her to show me around the campus and help me complete the admission formalities. She happily agreed and took me around the Hostel, Gurunath Stores, Academic Section, and the Student Facility Centre. We chatted as we walked all day and completed all the formalities. By the time we came back, my legs were aching, but my heart was brimming with happiness. Since then, we became best friends; I turned out to be the philosopher, and she, the guide!

It was wonderful to be amongst students half my age and study with them. The next generation was extremely intelligent and hardworking. However, I found them anxious about their future. Questions such as "Will I make it to my dream job?" and "Will I get an ideal life partner?" rattled their minds constantly. Some were facing parental pressure, while others were dealing with financial pressure. Oh my God! It was perhaps their age or the stage in life; they were facing **Quarter-Life Crisis** full on....

For coursework, we had to take a bunch of Finance and Economic courses and clear them. After that, we were staring at our next challenge – The Doctoral Committee Review. We had to submit a research proposal the next day. It was late at night, Kartika and I were glued to our computers for hours finalising our PPT in the small finance lab opposite our guide's room, which was packed with books and computers. The clock struck one. My spine went stiff, and feet felt crammed.

"Let's take a break," I suggested.

"Five more minutes, ma'am," she said, giving final touches to her presentation.

I got up, did some stretches, and walked in the corridor, waiting for Kartika. She closed her laptop, locked the room, and joined me.

We decided to take a walk from Gajendra Circle to the main gate. When we stepped out, the cool breeze blowing, relaxed our tired bodies. We ambled, absorbing the serenity of the night.

"Ma'am, look at the beautiful moon," she said, pointing at the sky.

'Wow!' I said, feeling exhilarated.

As we walked past the staff quarters, we saw a couple engaged in a warm embrace.

"Love birds!" she whispered. We both exchanged glances and giggled.

"At night, this campus turns into a lovers' park. You must check out the stadium," she said.

"Love is the most fundamental human need in the world, and this place is no exception," I pointed out. She nodded in agreement.

Somewhere, an owl hooted. The long roots of the banyan tree gave an eerie feeling in the night. As we continued walking, Kartika turned quiet. I turned to look at her and noticed that her eyes were moist.

"Are you crying?" I asked, surprised. I had never seen her low-spirited.

"You are the most happy-go-lucky girl on this campus. I have never seen tears in your eyes. What's troubling you? Tell me what the issue is," I probed as I sat her down on the roadside bench, wiping her tears with my dupatta.

"Ma'am I deleted my Facebook account," she said softly.

"That is such a terrible thing to do! Why did you do that?" I asked, raising my eyebrows, while in my mind, I was amused. My generation was not into social media, so I couldn't fathom that shutting an account was such a dreadful thing to do.

"Everyone I know has a boyfriend. They show off their boyfriend on social media. Right now, a couple of my friends are enjoying in a resort in Mahabalipuram, while I am slogging it out on the campus doing meaningless analysis for hours. I do not have a boyfriend, nor the time to post pics. That's why I shut the damn account," she sobbed.

"Ayyo!" I said, expressing concern. "It's OK not to have a boyfriend. In time, everything will change. Life will never be the same. You will meet the man of your destiny at the right time. You are such a beautiful girl; you must be having quite a few admirers," I consoled her, and she smiled.

"Ok, tell me, what kind of person do you want to marry? What are the qualities that he should have?" I asked, changing gears.

Kartika's eyes sparkled. "He must be tall and well-built, just like me, very handsome, well-qualified, and have a good job," she said.

"Hmm... believe it or not, your dream will come true, every bit of it, every detail will manifest. Tell me more about what you aspire for?"

"Ma'am, I want to become a successful corporate leader, earn money, and drive in swank cars. I want to live in style, in a beautiful apartment, travel outside the country, and most importantly, have love and support throughout my life," she said.

"Not everyone has such clarity about what they want from life. Since you are absolutely clear, it's just a matter of time. There is a time for everything in life. You have to be patient and hopeful while you work towards it and bide your time meaningfully. Since you have desired it, it'll manifest," I said soothingly. She felt much better. We went back to the finance lab to continue our grind.

Well! In a year's time, Kartika met Sumeet, a strikingly handsome engineer who was working in Dubai. It was love at first sight. They both got married, and she shifted to Dubai where she picked up a high-profile job as a finance researcher in a real estate firm. Yes, she drove to the office in a grand car. Soon, she got pregnant and delivered triplets, two girls and a boy, all healthy. By God's grace, Sumeet loves Kartika truly and supports her in all her endeavours. And yes! Finally, she opened an Instagram account and filled it with her family pics and videos.

Author Speak

Forever, this question rattled my mind, "Is our life scripted by the Universal Force or do we have the power to make our own destiny?" Many times, both seemed to be the case. Especially how we are born into a certain family or how we meet certain people in life seems predestined... But we can definitely shape our destiny, making the right choices in life, by education, hard work, upholding values, pursuing our passion, keeping hope alive, and waiting for the right time because there is a right time for everything in life!

03

FIRST CRUSH

... can be a fond memory ... but not to be confused with love forever ...

Among many others, Arjun Dev, Danny D'Costa, Vicky Ahuja, and Sia Raman studied at Zion's High School, Hyderabad. They were all in the final year at school. Arjun and Danny were in section 'A', while Sia and Vicky were in Section 'C'. It was the month of January, and with less than 3 months for their board exams to commence, there was tension among students and teachers alike.

The second hour was on in section 'A'. Ms. Bhawani was taking a class in Mathematics. She had told Arjun and Danny to leave the classroom as they had not submitted their homework. Final exams were due in about 3 months, but they were neither anxious about the impending exams nor were punishments new to them. Marching to the principal's office was their daily routine.

Arjun was happiest when he was playing sports. Sitting still in a classroom and listening to the teacher's lecture was the most difficult thing for him to endure. He would always sit in the last bench, make paper balls, and toss them at the front benchers. This would enrage the teachers, while he would be amused.

Danny was the naughtiest boy in class. He never paid attention to the teachers, would pick fights with other students, and often disrupt the class. He was a movie buff, and his classmates considered him to be an encyclopedia of information on Bollywood.

Arjun and Danny peeped into the classroom, "Miss, please let us come in. We will submit our work tomorrow." Ms. Bhavani was busy solving theorems on the blackboard. She turned towards them, anger writ all over her face. "Complete yesterday's work first, then you may enter the class!" she said firmly. Both of them looked at each other and went out again.

Ringg...! The school bell rang. Ms. Bhavani left. Arjun and Danny entered the classroom. A few minutes later, their class teacher, Ms. Pai, entered the room along with a few students. There was a noisy chaos in the room. "Silence, everyone!" commanded Ms. Pai in her strong voice. Everyone quietened. "We are shuffling students across sections to make study groups before the pre-final exams. This will help you all prepare better. Please welcome students from section "C," she announced. Everyone clapped. She settled the newcomers in their appropriate seats.

Vicky was asked to sit next to Danny. Danny was not amused at all. It was dislike at first sight. Danny tripped Vicky, and he stumbled. Other boys caught him, and he glared at Danny, who apologised with a smirk on his face.

Arjun noticed Sia as she was made to sit in front of him. He had seen her before when she was in the other section. She was very pretty, and her arrival infused a freshness into their otherwise boring classroom. His excitement rose as he tore a paper from his notebook, rolled it into a ball, and threw it at her. She turned back, looking annoyed.

Sia was a brilliant student. Hardworking and diligent, she would always submit her assignments on time. She aimed at getting top grades in her tenth board exams, and getting admission into the best college in town was her dream.

"Attention, everyone!" called out Ms. Pai and started marking important questions in the subject she taught. Everyone got busy noting them.

The bell rang, announcing lunchtime. Arjun ran up and patted Sia on her back.

"Don't you dare do that again," she warned him angrily.

"My hand hit you by mistake," said Arjun, with a naughty smile.

"You are a mischief-monger," she said, and walked away in a huff with her friends.

He laughed out loud.

That night, Arjun had a sweet feeling in his heart as he thought of Sia.

"Her eyes were so expressive, the delicate bridge of her nose, her soft lips, that prominent chin, and determined look on her face! Oh! She is so beautiful," he kept thinking. Was he in love? He wondered as he drifted into deep slumber.

Final exams were just one month away. As Arjun settled himself at his study desk, a heavy cloud of exhaustion descended upon him. The weight of textbooks felt like boulders; the mere thought of studying them drained him of all his energy. His phone rang, and the proposal of his mischievous friend, Danny, was announced over it.

"Hey Arjun! Why not escape the books and embark on a cinematic adventure?" Salman Khan's new movie has been released, and I have got two tickets for the afternoon show," Danny's voice echoed through the receiver, a tempting proposition filled the air.

This was an irresistible offer from the fun end. He hesitated momentarily, but the allure in surrendering to Danny's proposal took priority in his mind. Taking a quick decision, he shut his books and got dressed to go.

"Where are you going? Exams are just a month away," said his mother with a worried look on her face.

With a flicker of mischief in his eyes, he announced, "Ma, I'm heading for combined studies with my classmates. I will be back by 4 pm," he promised, as guilt gnawed at his heart for lying.

Arjun and Danny thoroughly enjoyed shouting comments and whistling at every dialogue in the movie hall. After the movie, they continued their outing and went to a nearby Irani Café.

Ordering two Masala Teas with Osmania biscuits, they felt really good. Discussing matters of life over a cup of tea, they felt like adults.

Danny said, "Do you know, Arjun, there's more to life than just exams and textbooks."

Arjun chuckled and said, "Yes, of course, like basketball, cricket, football, tennis...."

"And girls," added Danny, wistfully.

Arjun raised an eyebrow, a mixture of curiosity and amusement crossing his face.

He probed, "So, who's on your mind?"

Danny responded, "Vicky has an eye for Sia."

"How do you know?" asked Arjun, feeling disturbed.

"Just the vibes. He follows her without her knowledge. He is surely up to something," said Danny.

"But she is my girl! I am in love with her," confided Arjun self-righteously.

"Wow! That's fantastic!" "FWEET!" whistled Danny.

Arjun shushed him, his face turning red with embarrassment.

"We must do something about this Vicky guy. He is such a pain in the neck," he said, belting out some expletives.

Danny and Arjun continued their heart-to-heart conversation, their voices laced with anticipation, laughter, excitement, and intrigue. They delved deeper into the matter and got very angry with Vicky for having feelings for Sia. Their rendezvous came to an end, with them firmly deciding to watch Vicky closely for any further activity.

With the exams looming just 20 days away, Sia burned the midnight oil, engrossed in math problems at her home. As her mind wandered, she realised the school era was drawing to an end. Thoughts of summer vacation consumed her, but she couldn't help contemplating her results and future. Having toiled assiduously throughout the year, she exuded confidence to get merit grades in all the subjects. Her ultimate ambition was to crack the IIT-JEE exam and get admission to India's premium Engineering College. Her dreams didn't stop there... she longed for a future overseas, starting by doing a post-graduation, then research in her favourite subject 'computers'. Her wanderlust took hold of her as she yearned to explore every corner mentioned in her geography textbook: Europe, Africa, Australia, America, and yes, the icy realms of Antarctica too.

The world beckoned, and Sia's determination burned brighter with every thought.

While she was on this mind travel, the doorbell rang and interrupted her daydreams.

"Someone's at the door, Sia, go and check," said her mother from the kitchen.

Shaken from her reverie, she frowned as she opened the door.

Vicky, her classmate, was standing outside the door. She was surprised to see him.

"Hi!" he greeted her with a smile.

She did not know how to respond. She was not expecting him, or anyone else, to show up all of a sudden. This was very rude, she thought, and her mood got put off. Her expression became disapproving.

Her mother asked from inside who it was at the door.

"My classmate, Vicky," she muttered.

"Hi, Aunty. I am Vicky, Sia's classmate," said Vicky as he introduced himself and returned her book.

"Oh, okay!" said her mother, with a quizzical look on her face.

"Come in," she said politely.

Sia was confused initially, wondering why Vicky had come to meet her. Slowly, anger rose from the pit of her stomach, and she got enraged as he gave her the book in his hand.

"This is not my book," she said angrily.

"Oh, my gosh!" he said. There was an awkward silence.

"How are your preparations going?" he asked, breaking the silence and hoping to start a conversation.

"Well," she answered and pursed her lips. Another embarrassing pause ensued. Not knowing what to do, he got up and left, and she heaved a sigh of relief.

"Who is this fellow, Sia?" asked her mother.

"I never gave him my book. I have never, ever spoken to him in school. He just barged into our house. These are the rowdies who infest the last benches. Bloomin' rascal!" she said, seething with anger.

"It's okay! Don't use foul language. Let it be," said her mother, trying to calm her down.

With the exams only 10 days away, Arjun and Danny met again at the school office. They had come to collect their hall tickets.

"I have news for you, Vicky went to Sia's house," informed Danny.

"WHAT?" said Arjun, horrified. He could feel warm blood rushing into his brain. He wondered why Vicky had visited Sia and asked Danny the same.

"*Befkoof Ashique Saala!*" (Wannabe lover), swore Danny.

"How dare he?" fumed Arjun, grinding his teeth, and said, "*Nahee chodunga usko* (I won't leave him), he's gone too far."

"Take it easy, bro," said Danny, trying to calm him down.

"I have had my eyes on him for the last 3 months. He always hovers around Sia, waiting for an opportunity to grab her attention and talk to her. Irritating, bloody fellow! He is such a leech that he has the gall to go to her house directly. He deserves to be taught a lesson," fumed Arjun.

"I have a plan," said Danny, and whispered something into Arjun's ear.

"What a plan! That should give him a scare," agreed Arjun, feeling excited.

The countdown to the day of exams had started, and it was barely a week before the academic assessment storm would descend on them. But Arjun and Danny, unmindful of it, lay in wait for Vicky near their school canteen. The school grounds were fairly deserted, and they knew that Vicky visited the canteen every day at 5 pm after his tuition class got over.

The sun cast long shadows as Arjun and Danny donned dark glasses and wound scarves around their faces to hide their identities.

From a distance, the two saw Vicky stroll towards the canteen, unaware of what was brewing. They pounced upon him, like eagles do on a prey.

Vicky stumbled. He was confused as to what had hit him. By the time he realised, Arjun had already slapped him, and Danny had snatched his phone.

At the speed of light, Arjun and Danny escaped, leaving a shocked Vicky behind.

Vicky let all hell break loose as he had recognised them! He made a lot of noise, went home, and complained to his parents. They were enraged by this assault and decided to go to the police instead of the school principal.

Soon, Arjun and Danny's parents got summons from the police station. They were aghast at what their so-called prodigious offspring had got them into.

Time ticked on the clock. There were only three days for their exams to commence. Circle Inspector Vijay, in charge of the Zion police station, was seated in his room surrounded by Vicky, Arjun, Danny, and their respective parents. It was the most unpleasant moment of their lives as they all faced each other.

Inspector Vijay asked them, "Why did you both assault Vicky?"

Arjun stood frozen, too shaken to respond.

Vijay then asked Danny to tell what happened.

Danny confessed, "Sir, Arjun loves Sia, but Vicky is also interested in her. He has been following her, and he even went to her house. So, we confronted him."

"Ah! I see, a love triangle," exclaimed the Inspector, rolling his eyes. "I understand now," he declared with clarity.

Arjun's parents were consumed with anger and unleashed a torrent of admonishments, delivering a stinging slap on Arjun's cheek.

Vijay stopped them, saying, "No! Don't resort to violence. That's not the solution," he advised.

He turned to the boys and said, "I don't understand, what did you take his cell phone for?"

Arjun said defensively, "It wasn't part of the plan, Sir. Danny took it without thinking, and we both made our hasty escape."

Teary-eyed Arjun and Danny returned the cell phone to Vicky and apologised to all the people present at the police station.

Vijay asked them, "Do you realise what you have done?" and told them, "Assaulting someone and stealing his cell phone is a crime. Under IPC (Indian Penal Code) section 379A and U/s 352, it can lead to arrest and imprisonment. A criminal record can spoil your life forever." He softened his tone and continued, "You belong to good families. Do not try such stunts and damage your future. Go and prepare for your exams. Don't waste time."

He convinced Vicky's parents to withdraw the case, in light of the fact that all involved in the case were minors. He counselled the boys to study well and not get diverted to wrong ways.

Sia was shocked and stunned to learn that two boys had engaged in a brawl over her affections, unaware that she held no romantic feelings for either of them. She felt a mixture of sympathy for their misplaced passions and frustration at their lack of understanding. Their battle had unnecessarily dragged in her name, and she was very upset about it.

They were responsible for the chaos and disturbance caused just before board exams, and this overwhelmed her. She was extremely embarrassed about the whole incident as her parents came to know eventually. She did what she could, blocked all the boys off her social media account and decided not to see their faces ever in her life.

Author Speak

As we see in this story, both Arjun and Vicky are infatuated for the first time towards the same girl. She is interested in neither of them. They even get into blows, reach the police station, and endanger their future for this! Love is a beautiful emotion that all yearn for. The experience during teenage is also common to all, as all the hormones act up. It's natural to get attracted to someone. However, you are not yet ready to get into serious commitment. It requires a lot more maturity to be able to handle oneself and another individual at the same time. Now is the time to discover yourself and build a persona of your own. You don't find love... Love finds you... it all happens naturally...

MOTHER'S MOTHER

Caring for loved ones is a noble and virtuous act!

It was a Friday afternoon; the auditorium was packed to its maximum capacity with employees of Tech-Titan Company for their weekend human resource bonding programme "All-Hands Meet". Never was an HR[8] meet so popular before. They all waited with bated breath for Vice President Sunayna Rao to start the session. She walked in gracefully and ascended the stage. A hush fell in the hall as audiences gaped at her in admiration. Dressed in a grey and white suit, she had styled her sleek hair straight. Adjusting the mic to begin her address, she looked warmly at the audience with her sea-green catlike eyes; her charming smile lit up the assembly hall. "Good afternoon to all and welcome to All Hands Meet..." started Sunayna, and the hall reverberated with thunderous applause. She had an electrifying personality and the fitness of an athlete; with classical good looks, she was a spectacle to behold. Her session was full of fun games and activities, which were hugely appreciated. Employees looked forward to this refreshing weekend experience. Within a year of joining the firm, she had reduced the attrition rate by ten percent.

Among her many admirers in the audience was Rishi Sooryavanshi, the CFO of the Company. Dressed in an electric-blue shirt, beige chinos, and sand brown slip-ons, he looked dapper. His well-groomed beard highlighted his high cheekbones and square jawline. His slant sideburn added to his flamboyance. Starting his life as a rank holder Chartered Accountant, at the young age of forty, he had risen to becoming the Finance Director of this Tech giant firm. He was highly respected for his expertise and knowledge, which saved the day when another global conglomerate played foul and wanted to acquire their company by unfair means.

Sunayna's session came to an end. Rishi got onto the stage and took the mic from her, making some important announcements about company stock options and the procedure to invest in his deep voice. Euphoria erupted in the gathering as their company was doing very well, and the stocks were soaring in the markets.

The meeting ended, and the world moved on to another weekend. It was Friday night, and Rishi went back home to his loneliness. After a bath, he relaxed and decided to cook a one-pot meal for himself. Cooking was therapeutic. He decided to make Bisi-beli-bath (a hot veggie-lentil-rice). As he sliced and diced the vegetables, he got lost in his past.

His marriage to Anusha, his parallel rise in career, increase in international business travel, his inability to give her time, slipping into unhealthy eating and drinking habits during corporate dinners and parties, Anusha's protest, and her sudden exit from his life. Wounds of the heart became fresh again. The pain resurfaced.

A knock at his door broke his reverie. Varshini, his sister who lived next door, entered with some food. She came along with her five-year-old daughter, Pia.

"Mama..." called Pia and ran into his open arms.

"Hey, Pia," he said, picking her up.

"You are such a stress buster. The best way to spend a Friday evening is to play with you," he said affectionately.

"Anna, you must marry again. It's been ten years since you got divorced. Anusha has moved on. She got remarried and is the mother of two children now. Look at you! You have got stuck in time. I am anxious about you. Sometimes I suspect that you drink alone, then I lose sleep over your health," said Varshini, looking worried.

"I agree with you," said Rishi, with mischief in his eyes.

"Wow! For once, you agreed with me. Have you met someone? I can see it in your eyes. Tell me about her," urged his sister excitedly.

"Her name is Sunayna Rao. She works in my company as Vice President HR. She has done an MBA in Human Resources and a PhD in Psychology," elaborated Rishi.

"How does she look?" asked Varshini, shifting focus to her physicality.

"She has beautiful eyes. When she looks down, it seems the clouds overwhelm the wild blue yonder, but when she looks up, the sun is rising in the heavenly skies. When she looks at me, I drown in the green ocean of her eyes. Her smile is like the rainbow in the horizon. When she walks past, I feel the energy around her. She is absolutely divine," said Rishi dreamily.

"Oh! You are totally in love," observed Varshini with a bright smile.

"What's her family background?" she asked, probing further.

"She hails from the small town of Tenali in the state of Andhra Pradesh. Her father is a landlord, her mother a traditional homemaker, and she is a divorcee and a single mother."

"Oh, she has a kid!" exclaimed Varshini.

"That's all I know about her," stated Rishi, raising his hands and shrugging his shoulders.

"You must approach her at the earliest. Do not delay. Let not life pass by you once again," advised his sister as she left.

Zipping past a manic Monday, Rishi carried out back-to-back meetings with the finance and the planning teams. He gave detailed instructions to his PA about his week-long schedule and other reports. By 4 pm, he was exhausted. Sitting in his chair, he consciously slackened his breath. As his breath became slow and rhythmic, his mind became peaceful. He closed his eyes and visualised an ocean, where waves were lazily reaching the shore and then receding, making a rustling sound. The sea-gulls cawed as they glided in the sky. Suddenly, he had a vision of a woman dancing in flowing white clothes. She swayed gracefully, the wind played with her hair, she played with the waves, and turned towards Rishi; he saw those green eyes... drowned in them and then lost the vision.

He woke up with a start. His lips broadened into a smile. Getting up, he stretched himself, then walked past the office gate into the neighbouring Starbucks coffee house. 'Aah... a nice coffee will surely perk me up,' he thought.

Having ordered a Café Latte and a Southwestern veggie wrap, Rishi was waiting in the line to get his snack when he saw none other than Sunayna, along with her friend, join the queue. He smiled at her; she smiled back. He wished her, and she responded.

"May I order something for you?" he asked politely.

"Don't bother," she said with a curt smile, and started conversing with her friend.

Rishi moved away with his food to an empty table. He sat down to eat. From the corner of his eye, he noticed her. Oblivious to his presence, she was engrossed in a serious conversation with her friend.

Rishi finished his coffee and set down his cup with a light clink on the table. He stood up from his seat and made his way over to Sunayna's table, a small smile playing at the corners of his lips. "Hey, Sunayna," he said warmly, "I just wanted to say that your session on Friday was great. I really enjoyed it."

Sunayna looked up, pleasantly surprised to receive compliments from him. "Thank you, Rishi," she replied, her tone appreciative. "I'm glad you enjoyed it."

Rishi nodded, his eyes bright and friendly. "Yeah, I learned a lot," he said. "You really know your stuff. I was thinking maybe we could grab lunch sometime and chat more about it?"

Sunayna nodded and smiled. After a few seconds, she said, "Sure."

Rishi took leave and walked back to his office. He couldn't help but notice how beautiful Sunayna looked just then. Her hair was tied up in a ponytail, she was wearing a green salwar suit with silver hangings in her ear, and she radiated natural grace and poise. He felt a sudden surge of attraction towards her and wondered if this lunch might be the start of something more.

After Rishi left the coffee house, Sunayna and her friend Kaajal started chatting about him.

"Isn't he too fast?" complained Sunayna. "Can you believe he invited me for lunch?"

"That's not bad at all. He is a star performer. Watch my words, very soon he will become the CEO of this firm," predicted Kaajal.

"I think he is oversmart! I didn't like him butting into my session and grabbing the mic," complained Sunayna with a frown on her face.

"Don't be so harsh, Sunayna! I think he has feelings for you," claimed Kaajal with a cheeky smile.

"Don't tease me. I am not interested," retorted Sunayna.

Nevertheless, they kept talking about him until they reached the office.

It was the famous 'South Indian Bridal Fashion Week' at the five-star Novotel Hotel, all tickets were sold out. The who's who of the fashion world were attending along with the top film fraternity. Both Sunayna and Kaajal had managed to get seats in the first row.

The lights in the hall dimmed, and a silence fell over the audience as the emcee's voice boomed over the loudspeaker. "Ladies and gentlemen, the moment you've been waiting for has arrived - the bridal collection is about to be unveiled!" The crowd erupted in applause and cheered as the first model stepped onto the ramp.

She was dressed in a gorgeous ivory lehenga, her hair styled in loose waves that cascaded down her back. The intricate gold embroidery on her outfit shimmered under the bright lights, drawing gasps of awe from the audience. The model glided down the ramp with effortless grace, her eyes fixed ahead as if lost in a world of her own.

The next model followed close behind, dressed in a bright red sari with a heavy golden border. Her makeup was striking, with bold red lips and kohl-rimmed eyes, she sashayed down the runway, her hips swaying in time to the music, and the crowd broke into applause once again.

As the models continued to glide down the ramp, each more stunning than the other, the audience was mesmerised by the sheer beauty of the collection.

The show reached its climax as the showstopper Trishala stepped onto the ramp. Strikingly tall and confident, she was dressed in a breathtakingly beautiful pink bridal gown. The long gown trailed behind her as she glided on it, looking like a vision out of a fairy tale. The audience rose to their feet in a standing ovation as she turned and blew a kiss to the crowd.

Sunayna's face beamed with happiness as she watched her 20-year-old, beautiful daughter, Trishala, on stage. After the show ended, both Kaajal and Sunayna headed backstage to meet her.

"Hey... Trish," called Sunayna, stretching out her arms as she hugged her daughter in the green room.

"Wow! That was a great show," declared Kaajal.

"Thanks for coming, Aunty and Amma, you made my day," said a happy Trishala, busy removing her makeup.

It was past 10 o'clock at night. The city traffic had ebbed. Sitting behind the steering wheel of her car, Sunayna drove home with her daughter. There was a surge of pride in her heart as she glanced at Trishala. Her daughter was all grown up now, in her final year of engineering and doing modelling part-time; she was ready to take on the world.

A little while after reaching home and having dinner, Trishala sat across from Sunayna, a serious expression on her face. "Amma," she said, "I want to discuss something very important with you,"

"Yeah, what's up?" asked Sunayna, looking at her.

"I think it's time for you to move on. You need to give life another chance; you must marry again."

Sunayna looked at her daughter with scorn. "No! Not again. I am not discussing this topic. Don't you see that I am in a happy space? I want to discuss **your** plans, Trish. What are your future plans? Do you want to pursue modelling or go abroad to do a Masters in Computers?" questioned Sunayna, turning the tables.

"I am unable to plan my future because I am anxious about you, Amma. Until you decide on what you want to do with your life, I am not moving forward. You hardly had a marriage, and I was born too soon. You spent all your life working and looking after me single-handed. I think you deserve to have someone to share your life with, to love and to be loved in return. You deserve happiness. You're still so young and beautiful, and there are so many great guys out there in the world."

Sunayna smiled at her daughter's concern but shook her head gently. "I appreciate your concern, Trishala," she said, "you have been saying this since you were in grade six, but I am not sure yet."

"Well, I am making my efforts. I have registered your details in matrimony.com," said Trishala, dropping a bombshell.

"Oh! That won't work, sweetheart. It has to be someone very mature and understanding, someone spiritual. I am not sure such a person is registered on matrimony.com," said Sunayna, feeling uneasy.

"I am sure that someone is around and actually very near us. We need to identify him. He has to be an achiever, as brilliant as you, as good-looking as you," added Trishala with a twinkle in her eyes.

"Go to sleep. It's quite late; you must be very tired," said Sunayna, closing the topic.

That night, Trishala lay in her bed, staring up at the ceiling, lost in her thoughts. She couldn't help but think about her mother, Sunayna, and all that she had been through. She knew that her mother had been forced into an arranged marriage to a much older man when she was barely 18 years old. She had become pregnant the following year and had rebelled against the marriage, leaving her husband's house and starting all over on her own. Despite all the obstacles she faced, Sunayna had managed to rebuild her life, completing her education and raising Trishala as a single mother.

Sunayna had been a brilliant student. She dreamt of becoming an IAS officer. After completing her graduation, she had enrolled in a coaching centre and studied hard, even while she attended to Trishala, who was just a toddler. She cleared her prelims and mains in her first attempt. When she got her interview call, baby Trishala fell very sick. Sunayna decided to look after her daughter and missed the greatest opportunity of her life.

Trishala could imagine how difficult it must have been for her mother to sacrifice this for her, and felt a deep sense of respect and admiration for all that Sunayna had accomplished. As she lay there, Trishala vowed to herself that she would convince her mother to marry and start a life of her own. She would never forget her mother's sacrifice, strength, and resilience with which she had faced adversity.

A few days later...

Trishala burst into the living room where her mother, Sunayna, was sitting on the sofa, very excitedly.

"Mom, I bagged an internship at your firm, Tech Titans!" she said.

"Wow! That's wonderful news! Congratulations!" said Sunayna, beaming.

Trishala plopped down next to her mother and pulled out her laptop.

"I'm going to work as an intern under Rishi, the CFO. He's so amazing, Mom! I can't wait to learn from him," said Trishala.

"Rishi is very good in matters of finance. You will learn a lot. He's quite well-known in the industry," said Sunayna, nodding her head in appreciation.

"Do you know him, Mom?" asked Trishala.

"Yes, I know him. He is my colleague," said Sunayna, smiling. "He's actually been trying to reach out to me of late," she added bashfully.

Trishala raised her brow and looked at her mother in surprise.

"Wow! Tell me more about Rishi," she said, getting highly interested.

"Oh! That's a story for another day," smiled Sunayna wistfully. "Just remember, Trishala, don't tell anyone that you're my daughter while you're at Tech Titans," she cautioned her.

"Why not?" asked Trishala indignantly.

"That'll give you a fair ground to work and learn. People will be biased if they come to know," said Sunayna, breathing deeply.

"Okay, Ma," Trishala replied softly.

Trishala started her internship with Tech Titans, working with the business analytics team. She was excited to work with Rishi, the CFO. On the very first day, she went to the office, heads turned. She drew a lot of attention because of her unusual height of six feet, coloured hair, and a Buddha tattoo on her arm. Soon, she became popular among her team members because of her friendly, outgoing nature and youthful energy. She quickly proved herself and was even given the opportunity to participate in an important business meeting with Rishi's team, presenting key statistics to the group.

Throughout her internship, Trishala watched Rishi closely, wondering if he was the right person for her mother, Sunayna. She knew her mother was wary of Rishi, but Trishala couldn't help but feel drawn to him. As she worked alongside him, she found herself admiring his intelligence and drive. But she also noticed how he could be intense and demanding and wondered if he would be a good fit for Sunayna.

Despite her mixed feelings, Trishala continued to work hard and learn as much as she could during her internship. She knew that the experience would be valuable, regardless of what happened or didn't happen between Rishi and Sunayna.

Soon, her month-long internship came to an end. She was looking forward to her exit interview with Rishi.

The office assistant beckoned her to Rishi's office cabin. Rishi was not there. She noticed with interest that the walls were painted in a calming shade of light grey, while the floor was wooden. Large windows let in plenty of natural light and offered a view of the city skyline.

She was watching a few framed photos and awards on the wall when Rishi walked in, in his usual brisk manner.

"Hi," he said.

"Hi Rishi, thanks for meeting me for the exit interview," said Trishala, beaming.

"Of course, it was great having you on the team for the past month. How did you enjoy your internship?" he asked.

"I loved it. I had a great experience working with the business analytics team, and everyone was so welcoming," she said happily.

"That's great to hear. You really made an impact in our important business meeting by furnishing statistics," said Rishi.

"Thank you. I tried my best," said Trishala, feeling happy on being appreciated.

"So, what's next for you?" enquired Rishi.

"Well, I'm going back to college for my final year," she said.

"What are your future plans?" he asked.

"I want to complete my Masters in Computer Science from a good university in the USA," she said.

"Oh! So, you want to fly away to the west like all the youngsters do," exclaimed Rishi.

"No, I will return and start my own venture," she replied.

"I admire your clarity. Good luck!" he said, concluding the meeting.

"Thanks, Rishi," Trishala said, and continued, "Actually, there's something else I wanted to talk to you about – a personal matter."

"Sure, go ahead," he said.

"You see, Sunayna Rao, Vice President HR, is my mother," said Trishala.

"Oh, I see! I did not have any clue that you were Sunayna's daughter," he responded with surprise.

Trishala told him all about her mother's life as Rishi heard with rapt attention. She concluded by saying, "I believe it's time for her to consider marriage again. After a lot of convincing by me, she has agreed. I had applied on her behalf on matrimony.com. There, I came across your profile and I noticed that you had shown interest in the match...?"

"Oh yes, I am interested," he stated, nodding his head. He was a little embarrassed, though, discussing all this with her.

"I just wanted to let you know that my mother has been through a lot of difficulty in her life, and she deserves happiness," said Trishala.

"Of course!" said Rishi and nodded his head in agreement.

"Before we proceed with this proposal, I have a few questions to ask," continued Trishala, as her demeanour changed into a person in control.

Rishi was amazed at Trishala's confidence. He asked her to go ahead.

Trishala then asked him, "Why did you get divorced?"

Rishi explained his past in detail and concluded, "It was all my fault. I was young and ambitious. I focused more on my career and gave her no time. Eventually, she left," he sighed.

"I am sorry," she said genuinely.

"I have accepted it. She is happily married now, with two kids..." he said.

"Oh, ok!" paused Trishala and asked, "Do you smoke or drink?"

"I do not smoke. I used to drink socially. I will not hide from you that after my divorce, I started drinking every day to escape the pain. Soon,

I realised it led to severe depression and insomnia. Then I gave it up by practicing yoga and pranayama. My mother and sister helped me immensely during that period," Rishi revealed to her.

Trishala probed further, "Tell me about your family?"

Rishi was both amused and amazed at the way she was conducting the interview.

"My father died a few years ago. Now, I take care of my mother. She spends her time between our ancestral home at Gulbarga and with me in Hyderabad. My sister is happily married and has a 5-year-old daughter. She is a great emotional support to me and my next-door neighbour," he said.

"What are your hobbies?" she asked.

"I read good books. I love music. I play the guitar," Rishi answered.

Trishala exclaimed, "Wow! I didn't know this. You are so talented!" She said, very impressed with this news, and clapped her hands.

"This is the last question. What are your views on household chores management?" she asked.

Rishi would have burst out laughing, but he controlled himself and just smiled and said, "I believe that household chores must be divided equally between husband and wife. By the way, I am a good cook and will undertake to cook every day for Sunayna!"

Trishala was truly delighted. "Oh my God! That's wonderful. Well! I have a suggestion. You and my mother should meet and get to know each other," she suggested.

"I would love to," said Rishi, feeling ecstatic. He had been trying to reach out to Sunayna, but she had not been responding. He was fervently wishing this would work out, and now Trishala's intervention was Godsent. She is our destiny… he thought.

"I just want my mother to be happy," she said, her voice thick with emotion, as she held back her tears.

Rishi assured her, "She will be happy. You're a great daughter, Trishala," he complemented her as he rose and shook hands with her, giving her a warm hug.

"Thank you, Rishi. It was great working with you," said Trishala. She came out feeling very happy with this interaction.

Rishi was totally astonished at the way a twenty-year-old girl had interviewed him so boldly. He was full of admiration for Trishala, who cared so much about her mother and took on the role of her mother's mother in finding an appropriate groom for her. He was perspiring by the end of this unusual, yet pleasant, interaction.

Trishala persuaded her mother to meet Rishi and proposed Valentine's Day as the ideal day, and *Olive Bistro* as the perfect venue for their meeting. *Olive Bistro* was a charming restaurant situated on the scenic bank of Durgam Lake, where they served Mediterranean cuisine and created a romantic atmosphere.

On the D-Day, Trishala got excited and went through her mother's wardrobe, picking out clothes and discarding them as Sunayna watched her with amusement.

"No, not this one. Definitely not that. Hmm, maybe this?" went on Trishala.

"Trishala, I'm not sure I need to dress up so much for this," said Sunayna, doubtfully.

"Of course you do, Mom! It's Valentine's Day, and you're meeting Rishi for the first time. You have to look your best," said Trishala assertively.

Sunayna laughed and let her continue to fuss over her outfit.

Trishala finally said, "Okay, I think this will do. Let's do your makeup now."

It was noon time, draped in a beautiful pink chiffon sari with a matching brocade blouse, Sunayna entered the restaurant. She wore a delicate gold chain featuring a tiny diamond pendant around her neck, twinkling in the light as she moved. On her wrist, she wore a delicate shell bracelet. Her hair was left loose, falling in soft waves around her face and neck, with a few strands framing her face. Her minimal makeup highlighted her natural beauty, with a light pink lip gloss and subtle eye makeup. The scent of jasmine mist perfume wafted around her, adding a refreshing fragrance to her captivating presence.

Rishi sat at a table by the window, overlooking the serene Durgam Lake. He checked his watch nervously.

She spotted him waiting for her. Her heart raced, and she felt unsettled for a moment. He rose from his chair immediately.

Dressed in a casual white T-shirt and blue jeans, Rishi walked up to her and greeted her with a bouquet of red roses.

"You look absolutely stunning, Sunayna," he said, as she blushed and took a seat at the table.

"Thank you, Rishi. You look quite a dapper yourself," she responded.

They ordered food and engaged in a casual conversation, enjoying each other's company. Making small talk about the weather and office gossip, they finished their meal. Then, Rishi took a deep breath and looked into Sunayna's eyes.

"Sunayna, I am honest with you. I have strong feelings for you, and I want to be a part of your life. Will you give me a chance to become a father to Trishala?" he asked.

This hit Sunayna like a tsunami, and tears flowed down her eyes uncontrollably, even as she didn't want to make a scene.

"It's ok. Let the emotions flow; you are not alone now. I am with you day and night, through thick and thin," said Rishi as he stood up and moved closer to Sunayna, taking her hands in his.

"Rishi, you are a wonderful man, and I would be honoured to have you in my life," she replied.

"You have made me the happiest man in the world. I promise to love and cherish both you and Trishala for the rest of my life," he said.

Sunayna leaned in and embraced him tightly, feeling a sense of contentment that she had not felt in a long time.

And then Rishi and Sunayna got married. Trishala turned event manager during the wedding and helped in drawing up guest lists, shopping for wedding clothes and jewellery, decorations, the wedding feast, and other beautiful events. After the wedding, Trishala left for the USA to pursue a Masters in Computer Science while Rishi and Sunayana lived happily on......

Author Speak

Generally, mothers worry about their children. Here we find a daughter worried for her mother's future. The daughter successfully searches for a groom for her mother of her choice and settles her into matrimony. After which, she flies away to realise her own dreams. Taking responsibility for the lives of loved ones is a sign of great virtue. It builds character and strengthens one's personality.

05

ADRENALINE RUSH...BUT SAFETY FIRST

Think carefully before engaging in risky activities...

Shiv removed his glasses and took a break from studies. He had been solving physics problems for the last 3 hours now, preparing for the pre-finals that were to start in the coming week. Standing up, he stretched his body and walked out of his room into the balcony for some fresh air. His tall and wiry frame made him look fragile; his friends at college would joke that a strong gust of wind might blow him away. A smile spread on his face as he thought of them; they were one hell of a gang. There was never a dull moment with them around.

Stocky and bearded, Govind was the naughtiest in class. Rustic Raju had a great sense of humour; he would relax the otherwise formal atmosphere in class with his witty comments. Short and fair, Pankaj was the most boisterous of them all; teachers often found it hard to pin him down. Shiv was the tall and shy guy in the class. They were studying in grade 12, chasing the formidable dream of cracking the entrance exam to the Indian Institute of Technology, the most prestigious university in India. They believed they had the nerve and commitment to make their dreams come true. Classmates and best friends, they called themselves **the Super-Four.**

Shiv took the call as his cell phone started vibrating.

Govind had taken everyone on a conference call. "Hi, guys! How is the revision coming along?" he asked.

"Completed the first half of the portion, the last few chapters are difficult ra[9]," reported Raju.

"Even I am having a problem with the last chapters," admitted Pankaj.

"What about you, Shiv?" asked Pankaj.

"Second revision is underway," he reported, smiling sheepishly as he brushed aside his unruly hair.

"This is too much," complained Govind. "We are still struggling with our first revision."

They all started teasing him, and he couldn't help but smile and weakly defend himself.

"OK, guys, I have a plan. Tomorrow night, let's all meet at my place at 9 pm after dinner. Shiv will help us solve all the tough questions and clear our doubts. It's a night out, guys!" declared Govind.

"Dude, we are all banking on you!" said Govind to Shiv.

"What about your parents, won't they get disturbed?" asked Raju.

"My parents are out of station. The coast is clear!" said Govind, concluding the conversation.

Shiv's mother, Padma, was a well-known lawyer in the city; his father, Mr. Rama Rao, was a busy doctor. They lived in an upscale locality named Uma Nagar in Begumpet. After dinner was over, Padma was

---

9   *ra – to address colloquially*

clearing the table, finishing her tasks for the day, when Shiv informed her about his plan to study at night. She was surprised and raised her brow.

"Exams start on Monday, right? Don't you think this will strain you?" she asked.

"It won't be all night long. We will be done in 3 hours. Together, we will revise the difficult topics. Come on, it's Sunday tomorrow. I will be back first thing in the morning," said Shiv to convince her.

"OK, go ahead," she said reluctantly as she kissed his forehead. He was nothing like his peers, totally in control of himself, forever a step ahead of his class. She was so proud of him.

Shiv packed a portable rolling blackboard along with his books. He stuffed some chalk pieces into his pocket. Govind lived just 5 minutes away from his place in the next lane. Mulling over a plan on how to maximise the 3 hours of group study, he briefly stopped at the roadside store to buy a Dairy Milk chocolate for himself.

Everyone had reached Govind's house and were ready. Shiv came in last and took over. He first fixed the blackboard on the wall and then pulled out a piece of chalk from his pocket and started solving problems on the board. He had made a list of important questions that might be asked in the pre-finals. They all heard him in rapt attention, started working out problems, and asking doubts. Shiv answered patiently. By midnight, they were all done.

"Super session!" concluded Govind appreciatively. Everyone clapped. Pankaj surprised Shiv by holding him from behind and tried lifting him. Shiv protested; he was smiling and enjoying all the attention he got. It was late in the night. The clock struck one.

Raju paired his phone to the boombox through bluetooth and put on some music.

"Hey, reduce the volume *ra*, it's past midnight. Neighbours will get disturbed," admonished Govind.

"*Akali babu*[10]," said Raju, "I am hungry." Everyone was famished.

They raided the kitchen and found some munchies. They also found some coke in the fridge. These were enough to party. As they looked out of the window, they sighted a black SUV parked in their backyard.

"FWEET!" whistled Raju. "What is that?" They all went out to examine it.

"What a beauty! I never knew you had a KIA Seltos, boss," exclaimed a surprised Raju.

"We bought it recently," replied Govind proudly. "It has a 1.6-litre turbocharged engine, automatic gears, black exterior, red interiors, and automatic temperature adjustment in seats," he went on enthusiastically.

"Do you know how to drive?" asked Pankaj.

"Yes, of course! Let's go for a ride," suggested Govind. Raju and Pankaj shouted in excitement.

Shiv didn't like the idea, "*Oddu ra*[11]*!*" he protested.

"*Killjoy, ra nuvvu*[12]*!*" they all teased him.

"*Endukura bayapadthavu*[13]*? They asked him, "Why are you scared?"*

"Our minds have got heated up with all the studies, just for some fresh air ra," they all started pestering Shiv.

He was not feeling comfortable. He never liked moving away from the plan. They were so different, impulsive, unpredictable, and adventurous,

---

10 *Akali Babu - Hunger Men*
11 *Oddu ra – No (in Telugu)*
12 *Nuvvu – you (in Telugu)*
13 *Endukura bayapadthavu - why do you fear?*

yet together they all made a great foursome, and the bonhomie was great. He finally gave in, and they all got into the car with Govind at the wheel. Shiv sat in the front, while Pankaj and Raju sat behind.

Govind manoeuvred the car smoothly out of his backyard and soon they were driving through the city streets. Hyderabad looked so quiet and beautiful at night, with fewer people on the roads. They made their way to Madhapur, the financial district. Putting their heads out of the window, feeling the wind on their faces, the boys admired the dazzling skyscrapers and the lovely roads of the new city. Pankaj shouted in sheer excitement.

"Let's go to the road that leads to the Biodiversity Building. You'll find the famous Dosa Bandi, which caters to night creatures like us," suggested Raju.

Govind veered the car in that direction, and they all had a hearty midnight meal of idlis and Masala Dosas. Shiv had never been out in the middle of the night, nor had he eaten at this unearthly hour. This was exciting indeed! After they all had their fill, they laughed, joked, and made noise.

After getting back to their seats, they hit the road once again. At the Gachibowli crossroads, instead of turning left which led homewards, Govind turned right towards the outer ring road.

"Where are we going?" asked Shiv, surprised at the change in plan.

"On a long drive," declared Govind, ignoring his weak protests.

As the car picked up speed, Govind turned on the music. The volume was high, everyone was enjoying, and they urged him to drive faster again and again. The beats of the music brought them alive. They loved to feel the adrenaline rush and excitement that the speed and music offered. It was exciting and thrilling as well.

Trucks laden with heavy loads were entering the city. As they zoomed past a turn, a truck suddenly came onto the road from the service lane and collided. Their car flung into the air and crashed into the ground with a loud thud, then overturned.

Everyone was injured and groaning, still shocked at what had happened to them. Shiv was injured the most as he was sitting on the left side and the entire car fell on him. His entire side hurt, he was bleeding, and he couldn't move. It was 3 o'clock in the morning. He managed to call his mother and tell her about the accident. Padma and Ram panicked; they rushed to the accident spot, located the boys, arranged an ambulance, and shifted all of them to the hospital.

Eventually, a case was registered against Govind for driving without a licence and exceeding speed limits. Everyone got away with small cuts and scratches, while Shiv had multiple fractures. He was bedridden for a year and lost an academic year, after which his academics came to a pause.

His friends visited him regularly for a while but soon got busy in their pursuits. He sat at home, blank and depressed, for another year. Later, he passed grade 12 with economics and commerce subjects and proceeded to do Law. The accident dented the careers and health of all the four friends.

Author Speak

Many a time, teenagers and young adults have lost their lives in such sorts of incidents. Teenagers love excitement and take up risky activities. There is a deep need to be accepted by their peer group. In this story, Shiv gave in to peer pressure and went along on a drive despite not agreeing with the idea. He did not have the courage to say **no**. Govind drove the car without a licence, which is **illegal**.

Most teenagers consider exams, getting good grades, cracking entrance exams, securing admission into dream universities, and thereafter securing a job with a fat paycheck in campus placement as challenges of life. But real-life challenges are when you face a serious health breakdown, lose loved ones, experience heartbreak, face unemployment or financial crisis etc. These are times when you have to be courageous, pick yourself up, dust yourself off, and move forward!

Also, friends are important, but don't build your life around them or according to them – it's an unstable foundation. Lastly, do not succumb to peer pressure, make choices that uphold values of life that have stood the test of time...

06

THE GIRL ON THE BICYCLE

Adversity brings out the best in you!

Jyoti Kumari lived with her family in Sirhulli village located in Darbhanga district in the backward state of Bihar. She was fifteen years old but had to drop out of school as her family didn't have enough resources to support her education. Her mother worked in the Anganwadi[14], while her father, Mohan Paswan, had moved to Gurugram, a satellite city of New Delhi, in search of better employment opportunities. He earned his living as an e-rickshaw driver.

Jyoti helped her mother with household chores and looked after her four siblings. She loved cycling around the idyllic village streets, running small errands. People in her village were mainly engaged in agriculture, which brought poor returns. They were all waiting for good schools, proper drinking water supply, electricity, and roads to be provided to them. Youngsters like Jyoti were very interested in mobile phones, computer technology, and the internet. They were aware that technology could change their lives, but there was no easy access to it.

---

14 *Anganwadi-Child Development Service Centre*

In January 2020, Paswan met with an accident and broke his leg. He could barely walk. As soon as they got the news, Jyoti and her mother rushed to Gurugram. They found Paswan bedridden and in great pain. Taking up the cudgels, Jyoti's mom took charge of the kitchen while Jyoti looked after her father. After spending a few days together, the mother had to return to their village, back to her responsibilities, while Jyoti stayed on to support her father. She now took charge of all the household chores: cooking, washing, cleaning, and caring for her father.

One morning, Paswan opened his eyes as the sunlight streamed into his room from the window. He tried to sit on his bed but couldn't as he was in pain. His hips and legs hurt. Jyoti helped him stand and walk to the toilet. Later, she helped him settle down in a chair and offered him a cup of hot tea and a bun.

"I don't know how long this will go on. We are running out of money. I must go out for work today. Even if I get a couple of customers, it will help," he muttered with pain in his eyes and lines of worry on his forehead.

"You can't go out to work, Baba[15]. You need to see a doctor," suggested Jyothi.

"There's no money, beta[16]," he said remorsefully.

There was a loud knock on their door. Jyoti peeped out of the window; a potbellied, short-statured man in a lungi was standing outside. He was their landlord.

As she opened the door, he barged in and yelled, "GIVE YOUR DUES AND VACATE THE ROOM," followed by some expletives! Jyothi's face turned red with anger hearing his foul language.

Paswan rose with difficulty and pleaded his case. He explained his health and economic condition.

---

15 *Baba- father*
16 *beta- child*

"I DON'T WANT TO HEAR ANY MORE EXCUSES. VACATE THE ROOM. THIS IS YOUR LAST WARNING, OR I WILL KICK YOU OUT," he shouted.

He further threatened to cut off their electric connection, and left in a huff.

Life was getting tougher...

A strange disease called Covid-19 was fast engulfing the world. An outbreak of a pandemic was in progress. On the 24th of March, Prime Minister Narendra Modi was on television ordering a nationwide lockdown. Paswan and his daughter watched this on TV in their neighbouring shanty, along with all the people who lived around those slums.

Their hearts sank. Faces ridden with despair and confusion, they looked at each other. They realised that this lockdown would hit them hard economically. What about daily wage earners? What about auto-rickshaw drivers? What about migrant labourers? Domestic help? How would they survive this lockdown? Their minds were swirling with questions.

There was no chance of earning. Mohan realised they would soon run out of money. Both father and daughter could not sleep a wink that night. It was now a question of survival! The best thing to do was to return to their village, but how would they travel halfway across India with no buses or trains plying?

"Baba, I will take you home on a cycle. Let's buy a cycle with whatever money we have left," she urged.

"Beta, it's not four or five kilometres that you will carry me from here. It's thirteen hundred kilometres! How will we go?" he questioned.

"Baba, I am good at cycling. In Sirhulli, I cycle the whole day for errands. I have cycled even to the nearby district. Trust me because we have no other option," Jyothi insisted.

While Mohan thought the idea was ridiculous, he gave in, surrendering to her confidence.

They bought a simple bicycle with the last of their savings just before lockdown. On May 8, 2020, they set off, Jyoti at the handlebars, baba the pillion rider. She started pedalling from the outskirts of New Delhi on her way to Darbhanga, their home district, 1300 kms away.

It was the peak of summer, and the sun was shining in its complete intensity. Braving the oppressive heat and dust of the highway, with her father seated behind, Jyothi embarked on a difficult journey with a smile on her lips and hope in her heart.

Day one, she cycled from the morning till the afternoon, and then it started getting really hot. A heatwave lashed at them mercilessly. Taking a break under the shade of a large tree along the roadside, they sat down and ate their packed lunch of roti and pickles. The bottled water they were carrying refreshed them and prepared them for the next stretch of the journey. She started pedalling again. Determined to cover more distance, she went on till evening. Fatigue struck, and her legs ached. They halted at a petrol bunk and decided to rest there for the night.

Sleeping in the open, she could see the vast expanse of the inky sky. It was a full moon night. The silent, spectacular, star-studded night sky filled her heart with peace, knowing that she was taking her baba home. With a prayer on her lips and determination in her heart, she drifted off to sleep.

Next day, they got up early. She wanted to cover the maximum distance in the early hours. As they proceeded, on the roads, there were hundreds of workers with their families walking back home. The mood was sombre. They had lost their jobs. There was the threat of an unknown virus. Only one thought ruled their minds: "LET'S GET BACK HOME."

After the lockdown had been announced, thousands of migrant labourers and their families, desperate and penniless, poured out of big cities and trudged back to their native villages where they could rely on family networks to survive. News was pouring in that some simply collapsed while walking down the long and hot highways, dead from exhaustion, while some got crushed by trains, and others run over by trucks. Undeterred by such news, Jyothi cycled on.

Many times, water and food packets were distributed by volunteers of charitable organisations or individuals who had risen to the occasion, immensely helping the people walking homewards

Jyothi pedalled nearly hundred miles a day. It wasn't easy. Her father was heavy, and he was carrying a bag. Many times, they had little food to eat. They slept at gas stations and lived off the generosity of strangers.

Sitting under a tree by the roadside on day six, they saw a truck at the far end of the road. She stood up and waved her hand, asking for help. Thankfully, the truck driver obliged, and they got a lift for a short distance.

They had crossed the big city of Lucknow. Jyothi knew she had crossed the halfway mark. Feeling happy, she was cycling with confidence when they encountered a bunch of young boys.

"Heyyy... a young girl cycles, while an old man rides on the pillion," they laughed loudly, mocking them.

Their words hit like arrows and injured Paswan's heart. "Halt! Halt!" he said, and Jyothi slowed down to a stop.

"This is not right, Beta. You are lugging me around while I am just sitting behind, being a burden to you," he said as he wiped tears off his eyes.

"Baba, they do not know that you are wounded. Don't take their comments to heart," she consoled him wisely, brushing aside the humiliation.

A media team travelling along the highway noticed Jyothi and her father. They interviewed them. Her story appeared on Prime-Time news in all the News Channels. Appreciation and public interest poured in. But she was blissfully unaware of all this. With strength and grit, she weathered the sun and exhaustion. With hope and determination, she cycled single-mindedly and was nearing her hometown.

One afternoon, she noticed a few travellers resting under a roadside tree. She approached one of them and requested if she could borrow their cell phone to make a call. They obliged.

"Don't worry, Amma, I will get Baba home safely," she called and reassured her mother.

It was the last hundred km she had to cover. She braced herself and cycled at a steady pace. While her face glowed with self-belief, her legs and back ached tremendously. She was tired and hungry. When she reached closer to home and saw familiar terrain, her joy knew no bounds.

Her mother was waiting outside their home as she finally reached. There were tears in everyone's eyes. Family members, neighbours, near and dear ones gathered and clapped their hands at their arrival. They were full of appreciation for the brave daughter who brought her baba back home.

She was besieged by news reporters. Her mother convinced village elders and news reporters to leave her alone, and let her quarantine and rest at home as she was very exhausted.

Her father quarantined himself at the village centre, as was the rule for all workmen returning from the cities. A Government rule to stop the spread of the virus to the countryside!

After resting for a few days, she gave loads of interviews to news reporters. She received a call from the Cycling Federation of India. Convinced that she was made of the right stuff, Onkar Singh, the

Federation's Chairman, invited her to New Delhi for a tryout with the national cycle team.

As news of her achievement spread in the media, the Government of India offered her a cash prize and free education. Ivanka Trump praised her on her Twitter handle, and a renowned corporation offered her prize money.

Author Speak

This story of a teenager who showed extraordinary courage, strength, and determination to bring her father back to their village greatly moved me. There is abundant capacity hidden in each one of us. Unleash the power within for the right cause, and you will pleasantly surprise yourself.

And remember, courage is not the absence of fear, but action despite fear!

Source: Financial Express Online, Updated: May 29, 2020, 11:32 AM

BBC News, 25th May 2020

07

GIVE BACK TO NATURE

Planet Earth is our only habitat, let's keep it safe!

Setting the incline to two, Prasoon Trivedi, a charming and strong boy of twenty years, was running on the treadmill at top speed in his balcony, while Prashant, his younger brother, only nineteen, robust and handsome, was lifting weights. They had converted their balcony into a gym. Both were studying Civil Engineering at Chaitanya Bharathi Institute of Technology College of Engineering; their semester exams had just concluded, and they were unwinding.

Being fit was a Trivedi tradition. Their father, Mr. Rajeev Trivedi, a very senior officer in the Indian Police Service, was a sportsman and a champion. He had swum the English Channel, the Strait of Gibraltar, the Palk Strait, and the Godavari River, thereby breaking many records in swimming. He was also a marathon runner and a long-distance cyclist. Their mom too was an ace swimmer and a yoga practitioner.

They lived in the picturesque Pleasant Valley, which had the characteristic Deccan features of hillocks, valleys, boulders, and bushes.

From their balcony, they had a complete view of the canyon below and the hillock thereafter, which was part of the Police Battalion.

Stepping down from the treadmill, sipping his protein shake, Prasoon caught sight of police commandos practicing building intervention tactics by zip-lining from a point on the hilltop to a nearby building as part of their routine training. "Hey, get my binoculars," he asked Prashant, his voice full of excitement and urgency.

As he watched carefully through the binoculars, he could clearly see the trainees zipping across a wire, one by one. His brother seized the field glasses and eagerly looked at the men in action.

"I want to do that," declared Prashant. "Me first," asserted Prasoon. Reaching out for his phone, he dialled his father's number to seek permission. Anything sporty was always supported by their father. He granted it to them.

The boys hurried up the hillock and made their way to the team. Procuring permissions, the Commandant permitted them to join the activity. They were strapped, one after another, to a suspended cable and secured with the harness locks, and then left to gravity to do its bit.

Prasoon was flying, "FWEET!," he whistled in joy. With the wind on his face, he felt like a superhero whooshing away on the zip line. He had the bird's eye view of the landscape around. It was spectacular!

Prashant followed suit. He was grinning from ear to ear as he soared along the cable lines. After finishing the ride, he gave a high-five to his brother and exclaimed, "That was fun!"

"Words can't describe the feeling of that complete freedom you experience up there!" exclaimed Prasoon as they walked back home.

"Did you notice the view from the top?" asked Prashant.

"Yes, I did! OMG[17]! I could see the entire city. It was magnificent. We must go there again," answered Prasoon, his face red with excitement.

Next day, the boys were up and about early in the morning, gymming as usual on their balcony when their father joined them.

"I am going to the 7th Battalion, Dichpally on inspection duties for a couple of days. Will you guys join me?" he enquired.

"Yes, we are free this weekend. We'd love to join you. How are we going?" asked Prasoon.

"Cycle," replied their father, smiling coolly.

"Cycling?" questioned Prashant, raising his eyebrows. "That'll mean cycling hundred and seventy-five km, might take 8 hours," he stated.

"Pack up tonight. We leave at 4 am tomorrow," said their father, nonchalantly.

"Looks like another adventure awaits us," smiled Prashant as he winked at Prasoon.

When it came to their dad, they always expected the unexpected. In the summer of 2011, he had taken them to Rajamundry where he was first posted as Assistant Superintendent of Police. There, they all swam across River Godavari, a stretch of 3.2 km from Kovvur to Rajamundry.

"That was one of my best swims," said Prasoon, reminiscing fondly. "It was a hot summer morning, and the river felt so cool and refreshing," agreed Prashant, joining his brother in the memory.

The following morning, they started early. It was their first attempt at long-distance cycling. The highway from Hyderabad to Nizamabad had good roads. The countryside was lush green with flourishing

---

17 *OMG-Oh my God*

sugarcane fields. The roads were lined on both sides with bougainvillea in full bloom. The beauty of the rural outskirts was enchanting; they loved the experience and cycled for 8 hours. It was only when they reached that they realised how drained they were. On arrival, they were offered sweet and cool sugarcane juice, which was just the need of the hour. Soon, Prasoon felt numbness and tingling in his hands and fingers. It was the strain from long-distance cycling. The doctor diagnosed it as handlebar palsy (cyclist palsy). After a month of physiotherapy and electric nerve stimulation, he started feeling better again.

"It's time for a new challenge," declared Prasoon on a Sunday afternoon.

"How about going up the hill?" asked Prashant.

"I am in," he replied enthusiastically.

After tea, the boys, along with their father and Toffee, their pet Beagle, went up the hillock. When they got there, they saw one of the best views of Hyderabad from the edge of the knoll.

On one side stood tall buildings of the new city Madhapur. On the other side were the magnificent luxury homes on the undulating terrain of Jubilee Hills, alternating with the unique rock formations, which are a notable characteristic of the city, along with large tracts of greenery. Along with the slums of Bora Banda in their neighbourhood, they could also make out the silhouette of the faraway majestic Qutub Shahi tombs.

Prasoon was stunned by the beauty of this picturesque location. He was reminded of the infinity pool in the Novotel Hotel at Vizag. An idea was taking shape in the mind of this civil engineer. He thought it would be great to have **an infinity pool right there on the cliff edge with that view.**

Toffee ran ahead, excited, smelling every nook and corner. As they went ahead, they discovered a pile of trash. People around were throwing garbage there. This pained their father deeply. "Something must be done to stop people from dumping their waste here," he remarked pensively.

Walking further ahead, as the terrain sloped down, they arrived at a large deep pit. A lot of cut stones were lying around. "Looks like illegal quarrying is going on here," observed Prashant. "Yes, it is evident," agreed their father, stroking his chin thoughtfully.

The evening sun was rapidly setting, a gentle breeze caressed them, and without warning, it started drizzling. They hurried towards a huge old tree nearby and took shelter. As it rained, water pooled in two spots. Braving the rain, they did enjoy their walk downhill with Toffee running along the slope.

Late in the evening, as they all gathered around the dining table sipping hot tomato soup prepared by their mother, a discussion started about the hillock.

"What a view it was, Ma! Breathtaking!" exclaimed Prashant.

"Did you notice the contours of the landscape? We can create a water body right on the hilltop, overlooking the view of the city by building a dam," observed Prasoon.

"Fantastic idea! This will naturally discourage people from dumping garbage. It will also create an ecosystem for birds and fish," added Prashant.

"How about a garden around? Maybe a small podium for cultural activities," added Prasoon excitedly. His imagination was now soaring.

"The newly formed Telangana Government has just announced **Mission Kakatiya**[18]. The government is serious about rejuvenating irrigation tanks and lakes. You never know, they might support this idea," said Mr. Trivedi encouragingly.

---

18 *Uplifting River Krishna waters to irrigate Telangana fields. A project dedicated to rejuvenating irrigation tanks and lakes in Telangana.*

Stimulated by this idea taking shape in their minds, the boys hiked up to the hilltop the following evening. They walked around and saw the paths the water took down to the two depressions and how it pooled there. The catchment area had a natural slope into the two depressions. To understand the contours of the area better, they decided to get a contour survey done. This survey would give a clear picture of how the water would run off during and after rainfall.

Going up the hill had now become their favourite pastime. The survey report suggested that the reservoir they wanted to build would not be deep enough to sustain itself throughout the year. To make the lake hold more water, the height of the check-dam would have to be very high.

"We can place two barriers; it will hold more water," suggested Prashant, adopting a practical approach.

"Great idea, bro!" said Prasoon and gave him a high-five.

"Did you notice that these two depressions are in two different levels, as if they are two steps," he stated.

"Yes, of course! In order to maximise storage of water, it makes sense to make one check-dam around the first depression and then a second check-dam around the other. This will allow us to have two lakes, both about six-feet deep," figured Prashant out.

"Look at all the rough stones lying around. That should be enough to build a gravity check-dam," commented Prasoon with a smile, happy at the opportunity to apply their civil engineering knowledge to a live project that would **give back to nature**...

The men of the 1st Battalion of the Telangana State Special Police, under the supervision of the Trivedi boys, got to work. Right from cleaning the entire surface of both depressions with brooms to the stone-by-stone construction of the check dams, they were the backbone for the execution of this project. Check-dam 1, with the walkway on top of it, was made entirely using stones found on the site. The railings on top of it were also made out of scrap steel. The reinforcement bars inside check-dam two were salvaged from scrap as well. Efficient management of resources led to minimising cost and wastage.

Clean and Green campaigns were being conducted nationwide and statewide. It was the right time to execute the project. The boys organised a plantation drive around the reservoir and their catchment area. Their initiative and effort had caught the imagination and appreciation of the entire neighbourhood. The residents of Pleasant Valley came out in full force and participated in the plantation programme.

Two weeks before the predicted monsoon, the construction of both the check dams was completed. Summer of 2015 came to an end in June when dark clouds gathered, lightning flashed, thunder roared across the sky like a whip, heralding the onset of the monsoon. Wind whistled as the trees around started swaying, raindrops started a serenade with their pitter-patter, and the air was ripe with the pleasant, dewy petrichor. The boys had awaited this moment with bated breath. It rained copiously that season; the heavens had blessed the project. In about a month, the reservoirs filled up.

Mr. Trivedi procured fish from the Fisheries Department and released them in the twin lakes. They served two purposes: firstly, to eat algae and control its growth, and secondly, to act as food for birds, thereby attracting them there. This rainwater harvesting project transformed the place beyond recognition. **Twin Lakes on a hilltop from where one could see the most spectacular sunrise and sunset in Hyderabad.** People stopped throwing trash around and disposed them off responsibly in the bins provided. Illegal quarrying stopped, and the place metamorphosed into a picturesque viewpoint and hangout.

An inaugural function was organised to showcase the project to the officers and the neighbourhood. The chief guest appreciated the boys and highlighted the fact that Mother Nature has given us all that we need to survive, but very few give back to nature.

Everybody applauded the boys as they shyly made their way to the podium. "The twin lakes and the catchment area have become home to fish, turtles, water snakes, peacocks, kingfishers, cranes, cormorants, and more," declared the boys to a standing ovation, "the joy we experienced in doing this project is unparalleled," they stated.

Three Years Later.................

Prashant peered out of the window as the plane gathered speed and took off. The ground seemed to fall away, while the vehicles on the roads started to look like ants, the houses looked like matchboxes, and he could see green patches here and there. He was very excited to travel across the globe to meet his brother who had gone abroad after his graduation.

In the past three years, both had made their career choices. Prasoon had moved to the USA for higher studies and the better job opportunities that awaited him, while Prashant had chosen to live in India. He had secured employment in a local construction firm. They did not always see eye to eye but were always connected heart-to-heart.

"Life is the outcome of the choices we make," he thought philosophically.

Excitement was in the air as the brothers met in Newark Airport. Prasoon had planned an exciting itinerary for his brother's short stay in the United States of America.

"It's going to be New York City first, Hollywood next, and a hangout at Las Vegas," he said zestfully. Prashant was absolutely thrilled.

The next month was a rollercoaster ride.

Travelling through the tunnel under the Hudson River and then over the Washington Bridge, the boys were delighted with the experience.

New York City! True to its reputation, "The city that never sleeps!" was exhilarating, fast-paced, and unforgettable.

For their LA and Vegas trip, they went along with a bunch of friends. The boys' brigade had fun strolling the Hollywood Walk of Fame, trooping the Rodeo Street, checking high fashion and high brands, spotting the billion-dollar mansions of the rich and famous at Beverly Hills, and hanging out at Santa Monica pier.

Vegas was another experience altogether. For the first time, they experienced the dynamics of a casino. They played Roulette and Blackjack. Lost money, got tipsy, and then laughed all night.

Thus, time flew, and a beautiful trip was coming to an end. It was the day before Prashant was due to fly back to India. The boys decided to go to the cinema to watch a Telugu film called '**Bharat Ane Nenu**'. "Nothing like watching a Desi film on foreign land," they said to themselves. Equipped with beverages and snacks, they chilled out as the movie progressed. Predictably, the hero and the heroine broke into a song and dance sequence, and to their surprise, they were dancing on the lakeside which they had created.

"Hey, Dude! Did you see that?" asked Prasoon in excitement.

"Wow, I can't believe that the spot **we created** has turned into a preferred location for film shootings now," exclaimed an equally thrilled Prashant.

Their joy knew no bounds as they experienced a feeling of fulfilment in their hearts.

Prashant had to leave for India the next morning, so as soon as they reached home, he got busy packing. When he noticed that Prasoon was packing too.

"There is a surprise for you. I am coming along with you to India," said Prasoon with a broad smile on his face.

"Yes, I love this country. I love my job, I love the life here, but 'Saare Jahan se Achcha Hindustan humara[19].' I want to contribute to my motherland. There is lots to be done in India.

I have made two decisions: one, I will only work for green projects, and two, I will start an NGO[20] that will work towards environmental conservation.

Prashant's joy knew no bounds. A man of few words, he hugged his brother, and that said it all.

As the plane took off the next morning, seated beside his brother, Prasoon glanced out of the window. He saw the perfect buildings, manicured gardens, and huge malls grow smaller and smaller in size as the plane zoomed far up into the sky, homeward bound.

Deep in his heart, Prasoon knew he had made the right decision.

Author Speak

The world is ours to inherit and bequeath to posterity. We must respect and preserve nature, being its unique creation, as we say we are.

---

19 *The best place in the world is Hindustan.*
20 *NGO-Non Govt. Organisation.*

08

KONDA AND KUTTY

Being trustworthy is important to build a noble character!

Not very long ago, just before the dark clouds of the pandemic engulfed the world, there existed a realm of hope and ambition in the hearts of youngsters living in the upcoming city of Hyderabad, India, where among them was a young man named Siddharth Konda.

He was tall and muscular, with a gym-defined physique. His beard and moustache accentuated his rugged appearance, while his long, thick, and wavy hair cascaded like a waterfall, giving him an artistic look. His perfect nose bridge added a dash of elegance to his striking features that were very appealing. Behind his captivating smile and twinkling eyes lay a fervent dream that soared beyond the boundaries of his homeland.

His heart yearned to cross the oceans, to go to a distant land called Canada, where he envisioned his artistic aspirations taking flight amidst the enchanting world of animation. Little did he know that his journey would soon be put to the ultimate test, as destiny stood ready to shape his tale in ways he could have never imagined.

After his graduation, he realised, during a brief internship, that the key to unlocking boundless career prospects lay in pursuing an advanced course at a renowned university abroad. With unwavering determination, he embarked on a quest to conquer the qualifying IELTS [21]exam and meticulously crafted a portfolio showcasing his mastery of art, digital art, and short animation shots.

Seeking guidance, he approached Shashank, an admission consultant, who became the guiding star in shortlisting and applying to the perfect-fit colleges. Together, they set the stage for his grand odyssey towards a destiny painted in pixels and visualisation.

In February 2020, late in the night, in the soft glow of his computer screen, Konda sat engrossed browsing the net. As he checked his emails, his heart pounded with anticipation, for he was expecting his results that day. Among the mundane messages, one subject line stood out like a beacon of hope: "Congratulations on your acceptance to Vancouver School of Arts!"

Emotions overwhelmed him as he clicked to open the email. His hands trembled, his eyes widened in disbelief. A euphoric joy erupted from the depths of his being. Voila! He had made it! Full of excitement, he ran down the stairs to share this happy news with his parents.

"Ma, Pa! I have amazing news!" he exclaimed joyfully. I have been accepted into the Vancouver School of Arts for Advanced Animation!"

"Congratulations, dear! We're so proud of you," said his mother, who embraced him warmly and kissed his forehead.

"Well done, my son! This is a big achievement," agreed his father, smiling from ear to ear as he hugged him.

"The course starts in the beginning of May, but I plan to leave by late April to settle in," said Siddharth.

---

21   *IELTS – International English Language Testing System*

In the ensuing month of March, Siddharth cleared his medical exam, secured the Canadian visa, and finished packing for his upcoming travel. His parents gifted him a brand-new computer packed with the latest features. Full of excitement and anticipation, he eagerly awaited his journey.

However, as fate would have it, by the end of the month, the world was shaken by an unforeseen event. A pandemic was declared, and suddenly, everything came to a standstill. Fear permeated the air as people retreated to the safety of their homes, avoiding contact with one another to prevent the spread of the dreaded COVID-19. To Siddharth's dismay, countries closed their borders, and flights were suspended, shattering his dreams. He was utterly shocked and deeply disappointed as his plans came to an anticlimactic halt.

Soon, he received an email from his college informing him that his course would commence online from September onwards. The initial idea was to learn by physically attending a foreign university and experiencing life there; this online arrangement could never fully replicate the offline experience. However, as an optimist, he pulled himself up from the abysmal situation and embraced a positive outlook.

Come September, and Siddharth's online classes started. India being in the opposite time zone of Canada, he started attending classes all night and tried to sleep in the day. Slowly, he warmed up to his professors and classmates and started enjoying his classes. His classroom was truly global. His classmates were from all over Europe, America, Australia, Asia, Africa, and India.

He took a liking to one of his classmates named Siddharth Kutty, his namesake. Passionate about art and animation, Kutty was creative, hardworking, and above all, a very helpful guy. That's what Konda liked most about him.

Kutty was 3 years older than him. Slowly, he assumed the role of an elder brother and helped Konda in all the difficult assignments and submissions.

Apart from coursework, Professors and classmates, Konda and Kutty chatted every day about their families, friends, hobbies and interests. They also shared what happened in the day with each other. They talked about their future in Vancouver over audio and video calls.

Konda discovered that Kutty belonged to a business family from Trivandrum. He was tall and lanky and sported a well-groomed beard, just like him. Kutty had a religious bent of mind and visited temples regularly. He was a strict vegetarian and a home bird.

Konda, on the other hand, loved non-vegetarian food, adventure, and was an outdoor person. He believed in God, but was not a regular visitor to temples . However, he liked everything about Kutty and cherished this friendship. He looked forward to being his roommate in Vancouver.

In the next eight months, they completed two terms of their course online. Two terrible waves of Covid had swept the earth, taking many lives. Numerous livelihoods had been destroyed, and many lives had been threatened. Slowly but cautiously, countries opened borders with restrictions. Canada started allowing students entering from abroad, with a mandatory condition that they quarantine in a third country for three to fourteen days. Some students chose to reach Canada via Mexico. Some chose Dubai; the easiest route for Indian students was through the Maldives.

It was May 2021. Both Konda and Kutty planned to travel together and reach Vancouver via Maldives by September 2021, as did many of their classmates worldwide. They hoped for an offline interaction and college experience the following year before the course ended.

Flight tickets costs had skyrocketed. Konda checked the travel costs. Each ticket was close to two lakh rupees, and the Maldives three days stay cost another lakh of rupees. Kutty's parents were shocked at the high price of the ticket. Konda was keen to travel along with Kutty, so he offered to book both their tickets together. He lied to Kutty that the tickets plus Maldives stay cost only two lakh rupees per head. He convinced his parents to take the burden of one lakh rupees on themselves.

After a lot of deliberation, Kutty's parents agreed. Their tickets were booked for the first week of September. Now, the shores of Vancouver seemed closer. Konda dreamt of a seashore, mountains, snow, and lakes that night.

He called Kutty early the next morning, "Hey, where had you been yesterday?"

"I went to apply for my Canada visa and clear the mandatory medical examination," replied Kutty.

"I cleared my medicals and got my visa last year," said Konda confidently.

Kutty got concerned. "Then your medicals must have lapsed by now."

"Oh no! Is the validity for just a year?" questioned Konda, getting worried.

"I didn't know this; it seems like I have overlooked it. I need to get my medicals cleared again, and without a valid visa, I can't travel," he continued anxiously.

Kutty asked Konda to take a deep breath and write to the authorities to explain his situation. He suggested that they might help in some way.

"Yeah, you're right. I'll contact the embassy first thing today. It's all happening so close to our travel date; I'm really tense now," said Konda, feeling nervous.

"Stay positive, my friend. Hopefully, everything will work out in your favour. We'll travel together and on the same date as planned," said Kutty encouragingly.

Konda hurried and once again cleared his medicals in the following week but was not sure it would reflect on the website by the time he travelled. Mentally, he strengthened himself and decided to leave it to destiny.

Come September, Konda boarded the flight to Trivandrum and met Kutty for the first time. Two tall, young men embraced each other as they united to journey forward.

They took a connecting flight and reached the Maldives. After a long wait in the immigration line and filling in an exhaustive online form with all their details, furnishing their Covid vaccination certificates, along with a hundred others, they were let into the island heaven for a three-day sojourn.

Maldives welcomed them with kaleidoscopic hues of blue and bright sunlight, while a gentle breeze was constantly blowing. Their accommodation was in an island resort. It was paradise with golden sand between their toes and turquoise blue water extending to infinity. A sumptuous, elaborate seaside breakfast bouquet was included in their package. They ate heartily and strolled along the shoreline, talking excitedly about the endless possibilities that lay ahead in the future.

With nightfall, the place got even more dramatic and romantic. They noticed that a number of young couples had flooded the place. It seemed to be a favourite honeymoon destination. Kutty and Konda relaxed after many months and cherished every moment together.

The shadow of uncertainty clouded Konda's mind that night. "What if the medicals don't show up in the website as cleared?" He would have to return to India, while Kutty would proceed to Canada the next day.

Early next morning, Konda got up and checked the Canada immigration website. Lo and behold! His medicals had been cleared. He was good to go. He woke up Kutty and shared the good news. He jumped on the bed in excitement, and Kutty laughed. Konda called home and shared the good news with his parents.

They had a late brunch that day and eagerly awaited the evening. Packing their luggage, they boarded a boat that sailed towards the main island where the airport was situated.

Konda stood behind Kutty in the immigration line. It was a long queue. After an hour or so, Kutty reached the counter. Kutty showed them all his documents, including a letter for admission to the college, Covid vaccination certificates etc. The officer asked for a letter from the college to the Canadian Embassy stating that the student was coming to Canada to attend term four. This was a bouncer. Kutty drew a blank. Immediately, Konda called their college Vice Principal, Mr Diwaker, and explained the situation.

Mr Diwaker was very upset. "You guys have to inform the college that you are coming and seek this letter well in advance," he grumbled, but quickly texted the required letter.

The immigration officer was heavily built, moustached, and had bloodshot eyes. He looked fierce. "Show me your term fee receipt," he shouted, losing patience. Kutty logged into his computer, accessed his college account, and pulled out his fee receipt, then stumbled ahead with his boarding pass.

Watching all this, Konda turned blank. The demeanour of the immigration officer was very intimidating. Konda's scrutiny started. He showed the officer all his papers.

"Where is your college letter to the embassy? Where is your fee receipt?" bellowed the cantankerous officer. He made Konda stand aside and started checking others in the line, sending them ahead.

Konda called his Vice Principal again for the letter. He shouted at him yet again and said he would send the letter. Konda tried opening his computer to log into his student account to pull out his fee receipt, but bad internet did not let him.

Time was ticking. Kutty had left him and boarded the flight. The entire line of passengers went ahead. The final call was heard. The immigration officer was unrelenting, and the flight left without Konda. His Vice Principal texted the required letter after the flight left.

Numbed with shock, Konda did not know what to do. It was a small airport. Everybody left. The airport became deserted as it was the last flight. Konda's papers and passport lay scattered on the immigration desk.

A local man approached Konda and said, "Looks like you missed your flight. You will need a hotel accommodation for the night. I will take you to a good hotel," he grinned wickedly. His teeth were missing.

Konda's heart sank. Realising that the next logical thing was to spend the night, he agreed and followed the dubious fellow, leaving his passport on the immigration table.

The malicious stranger led Konda through twists and turns of the streets and led him to a lonely, shady building. There was no one at the counter. He rang the bell, and an old man walked in. They both signalled each other and asked Konda to pay $500 for one night.

Konda paid them the money and checked into the hotel room. He shut the door and broke down. He sobbed all alone.

As the flight took off, Kutty's conscience had a huge pang of guilt. He had broken Konda's trust. He felt very bad about not helping him through the immigration process. 'If only I had done for Konda what he did for me,' he thought and felt a knot in his heart and deep regrets...

Being a strongly positive person, Konda recovered fast from the downturn. He lodged a complaint with the Indian Embassy, secured his passport, and flew back to India the next day. A fortnight later, he travelled once again through Dubai and Toronto and reached Vancouver successfully a month later. The immigration officer at Toronto stamped his student visa for one year as Kutty waited outside to receive him.

Because of his nobility, Konda did not hold anything against Kutty in his heart, and they resumed their friendship.

Author Speak

Trust and reputation have to be handled with care. Like glass, it can crash easily, but it takes a noble person and a world of effort to protect and preserve them.

Life is always uncertain. It is bound to spring surprises. We must move forward with courage and positivity, no matter what happens.

09

MYRA'S ODYSSEY

"The greatest glory in living lies not in never falling, but in rising every time we fall." – Nelson Mandela

In the charming town of Richmond, Virginia, where the James River flows gently through the heart of the city, Myra stood at that perfect height between tall and short, her wheat-coloured skin glowing with the warmth of youth. Her almond-shaped eyes, deep and expressive, captured the world around her with a quiet confidence. At just sixteen, Myra was a bright star, her talents blossoming like a garden in full bloom. Her fingers danced effortlessly over guitar strings, and her feet moved with a natural grace that captivated anyone who watched. With a heart brimming with kindness and a smile that could banish the darkest shadows, Myra was the star of every gathering, cherished by friends at school and in her neighbourhood. Meanwhile, her parents, two busy IT[22] professionals, worked tirelessly to provide for their family, often missing out on the beautiful moments of their daughter's journey. But Myra's constant companion, her loyal

---

Shih Tzu 'Coco', was always by her side, tail wagging, eyes shining with adoration.

As the calendar flipped to 2020, a sudden gust of change swept through Myra's life. Her father shifted his job, and they had to move to South Houston, Texas, a place where the skies were big, and the hearts were bigger. But for Myra, the thought of leaving behind the familiar streets of Richmond, the comforting embrace of her friends, and the school where she had grown from a shy girl to a confident young woman, was akin to tearing out a part of her soul. As the family packed up their lives into boxes and said goodbye to the only home she had ever known, Myra felt like a tree pulled out of the earth, her roots dangling in the air. Only one constant remained - Coco, her loyal Shih Tzu, who gazed up at her with big brown eyes, as if to say, "I'm here, with you. We'll weather this storm together."

Laughter and tears entwined as the family unpacked their lives into a new, independent home in Houston, a blank canvas waiting to be filled with memories. Myra, still reeling from the sudden displacement, tentatively stepped into a nearby school, her heart fluttering like a bird in a new cage. But just as she began to spread her wings, the Covid lockdown swooped in, casting a shadow over the city like a dark cloud. Myra's world shrunk to the four walls of her new home, her isolation a heavy chain around her heart. The silence was deafening, punctuated only by the soft whimpering of Coco, her loyal companion, who sensed her distress and nuzzled her hand.

As the lockdown tightened its grip, Myra's home became a battleground. The walls echoed with the discordant voices of her parents, their arguments over job security, career ambitions, and the weight of domestic duties festering like an open wound. The air grew thick with tension, each day a fresh skirmish, each night a fragile truce. Myra, caught in the crossfire, felt her heart tremble like a leaf in an autumn storm. She and Coco, her faithful confidant, became an island of two clinging to each other as the tempest raged on.

Haunting months of isolation had Myra teetering on the edge of sanity. But then, like a gentle breeze on a summer's day, online classes whispered a promise of connection, of community. As she delved into this virtual world, Myra discovered a mirror reflecting a stranger - two inches taller, hormones raging like a wildfire, and a soul bursting with vibrant dreams. She felt different and new. She yearned to paint her hair with the vibrant hues of a sunset, to adorn her nose with a glint of rebellion, and put makeup on her face. But her parents frowned upon her aspirations, urging her to tame her spirit and focus on studies. Myra felt frustrated and found solace in Coco. She poured out her woes, and Coco, seemed to say, "I get it, dear one. You're a canvas of colours, and I'll be your safe haven."

As the school gates creaked open, signalling the return of offline classes, Myra stepped into a swirl of classmates, feeling like a bird set free. Yet, amidst the lively chatter and familiar faces, she felt more like a piece of a puzzle that didn't belong. The popular girls, with their porcelain skin, emerald eyes, and golden hair, dazzled like stars, making Myra feel overshadowed by their brilliance. Her own reflection—marred by a constellation of pimples, oily brown skin, and a petite stature—seemed a cruel contrast.

But it wasn't just the girls who made her feel out of place. What cut her deepest was the way the boys in her class seemed to look right through her, as if she were invisible. Their laughter and camaraderie all passed her by as though she didn't exist. Myra's heart sank every time their eyes slid over her without recognition, as if she were a ghost haunting the room rather than a living, breathing classmate. The sting of being ignored gnawed at her, leaving her feeling small and insignificant.

Determined not to let this agony consume her, she resolved to change things. Sensing her determination, Coco, her faithful companion, licked her hand, offering silent encouragement, as she steeled herself for the challenge ahead.

In the treacherous landscape of high school hierarchy, Sophia and Isabella reigned supreme. Their beauty, confidence, and cunning forged an unbreakable bond between them. Like rival queens, they ruled with an iron fist, their inner circles coveted by all.

Desperate to get into Sophie's inner circle, Myra attempted to curry favour by whispering secrets about Isabella. But Sophia refused to believe it. Undeterred, Myra resorted to deceit, recording Isabella's voice on her cell phone on the sly and presented it to Sophia like a sacrificial offering. All hell broke loose when the very next day, both Sophia and Isabella confronted her, asking her why she played such a dirty trick. The consequences were brutal: ostracism, ridicule, and the scarlet letter of shame. Social media, that cruel amplifier, transformed her mistake into a spectacle, as #MyraHate groups sprouted like venomous mushrooms on Instagram and TikTok, their vitriol forever etching her name in the annals of high school infamy.

Myra's started an account on TikTok and unleashed her deepest struggles to the world. With each post, she exorcised her demons: the suffocating pressure of school, the numbing indifference of her parents, and the crippling self-doubt that haunted her. But amidst the anguish, she found solace in the creative expression of dance and music, her guitar melodies and rhythmic moves weaving a tapestry of hope. Her followers on social media started increasing steadily. However, her parents, oblivious to the turmoil, stumbled upon her online confessional, and her mother's fury ignited like a wildfire. "Delete your account," they thundered, but Myra, now a defiant storyteller, refused to silence her voice. The battle lines were drawn, a generational clash of wills, as Myra fought to reclaim her narrative, her identity, and her right to be heard.

Myra's once razor-sharp mind had dulled, leaving her struggling with science and maths. The textbooks that once felt familiar now seemed like Greek and Latin. The classroom, once a place of learning, became unbearable, and Myra often hid in the washroom to escape.

Soon, her teachers noticed her absence and informed her parents. Her mother, once proud of her achievements, now saw only a shadow of the bright student Myra used to be. The loss of Myra's brilliance was heart-breaking, and the fear that she might be succumbing to darker temptations made her parents feel deeply worried.

One day as Myra was walking back from school, she noticed a skating rink alive with the pulsing rhythm of youthful laughter. The air was electric with the thrill of freedom, as boys and girls glided effortlessly across the polished floor. The boys' rugged, inked skin and metallic accents seemed to gleam with a rebellious charm, while the girls' bold, pierced brows and navels sparkled like diamonds. Myra's heart yearned to join this carefree gang, to bask in the warmth of their camaraderie and unbridled joy. But her mother's stern voice echoed in her mind, a warning to steer clear of these perceived misfits. "They're trouble," she cautioned, her imagination running wild with visions of drug-addled delinquents, homeless drifters, and reckless thrill-seekers. The allure of the skating rink, however, only intensified Myra's desire to break free from her mother's suffocating fears and join the whirlwind of laughter and friendship that beckoned her.

One weekend, Myra accompanied her mother on a shopping trip to the downtown mall. As they strolled through the area, she spotted the same group of young people she had seen earlier at the skating rink. They were gathered by the roadside, exuding a carefree vibe as they played guitar and socialised. She noticed that one of them was smoking the hookah. They looked cool, and Myra couldn't help but feel drawn to their charismatic energy.

Under the veil of darkness, Myra's desperation for connection ignited a daring escape. One night, she ensured her parents' slumber, then scaled the treacherous terrain of the rooftop, her feet bare and her heart racing. With each leap, she shed the shackles of her isolation until she landed with a soft thud on the garage roof. The night air pulsed with rebellion as she snatched the car keys and unleashed the beast of her father's vehicle. The engine roared to life, a metallic heartbeat that synchronised with her own.

With a thrill-seeker's grin, Myra sped into the night, heading towards the rendezvous point where the homeless teenagers gathered. As she pulled up to the bridge, she leaned out of the window, her excitement evident. "Hey, guys! Mind if I join you?" she called out with a bright smile.

The group, perched on the wall near the bridge, looked up in surprise. "Whoa, a new face! What brings you here?" Sohael asked, his curiosity piqued.

"I saw you guys at the skating rink and downtown. I thought you looked like a lot of fun. Can I be friends with you?" asked Myra, smiling brightly.

"Yaaas, the more, the merrier! We don't get many newbies here," said Zoe excitedly.

"Especially not ones who show up in a sweet ride like that. What's your name?" asked Mason, grinning.

"I'm Myra," she said, as she hi-fived them all.

"Hey, Myra! We're Zoe, Sohael, Mason, Jake, and Eva. Welcome to the crew!" said Zoe, welcoming her into the pack.

"Yeah, we don't usually get people who want to hang out with us. You're brave, I like that," said Jake, high-fiving Myra.

"Or crazy. Either way, we're glad you're here!" said Eva, laughing.

They all shared a laugh, and Myra felt a sense of belonging.

"Thanks, guys. I feel like I've found my tribe," said Myra, smiling.

"Well, you've definitely found your partner in crime. Buckle up, Myra!" said Sohael with a smirk.

The wind whipped her hair into a frenzy as she merged with their tribe, her laughter and tears intertwining with theirs. Together, they embarked on a joyride to Jersey Village, the deserted streets their playground. At 3 am, they danced under the stars, their footsteps echoing off the silence. Myra's innocence was lost in the haze of her first smoke, the burn of alcohol on her lips and the rush of freedom in her veins.

But as dawn's pale light crept over the horizon, Myra's adventure came to an end, and she drove back home. Her father was standing like a sentinel outside their home, waiting for her.

"Myra, where on earth did you go driving out in the middle of the night?" he shouted furiously.

Myra felt her legs shaking in panic. Her mother emerged from inside, with her hands on her hips.

"Do you even realise how dangerous that was? What were you thinking? You don't even have a driving licence!" she said, her voice quivering with fury.

Myra's anger burst out like a volcano, "What was I thinking? I'm sick of this place! This house feels like a jail, and you two—you're like jailers! I have no freedom, no life of my own!" she screamed, her eyes blazing.

Stunned and taken aback, her mother's voice softened as she said, "Myra, that's not fair. We only want what's best for you"—but before she could finish, tears began to stream down her cheeks.

Cutting her off, Myra screamed, her voice shaking with emotion, "What's best for me? Locking me up, controlling everything I do? I can't breathe in this house!"

Coco was whimpering, sensing the tension, and stood by Myra, his eyes wide and miserable.

"Myra, we just worry about you. You're too young to understand," said her dad, trying his best to maintain his composure.

Myra stomped inside the house. She opened her almirah and grabbed her clothes, shoving them into a bag. She said, "Enough! I'm leaving! I can't live like this anymore!"

Sensing the escalation, Coco started barking frantically, his eyes darting between Myra and her parents.

Shocked by her reaction and realising they've pushed too far, her mother softened her voice and pleaded, "Myra, wait... Myra, wait..." she was softly crying.

In a bid to defuse the situation and prevent it from escalating, Myra's dad gently said, "We're sorry. We didn't mean to make you feel this way. Please, don't go. We'll listen to you, really listen." His voice was heavy with regret as he stepped in front of her, blocking her from leaving the house.

"Please stay. We promise to see things from your side," her mother pleaded, her voice full of earnestness.

Myra fell silent, her thoughts tangled in the tension between her anger and the sincerity in her parents' voices. She hesitated, her gaze shifting down to Coco, who was still barking, then back to her parents. Slowly, the intensity of her anger began to wane, replaced by a flicker of uncertainty. Sensing the change in her, Coco quieted, his bark fading into a soft whine. He nudged her leg gently, as if trying to offer her comfort in the midst of her confusion.

Myra took a deep breath, calming herself before grabbing her bag and heading back to her room, with Coco following closely behind. "I'm staying back only for Coco's sake," she muttered, before slamming the door behind her.

Mom and Dad shared a relieved glance, each silently promising to do better, to truly understand their daughter and her feelings.

The family, feeling the weight of unspoken tensions, decided to escape to Galveston, a serene beach town, hoping the open road and the sound of the waves would help them untangle the knots in their hearts.

As the miles rolled by, so did their guarded emotions. They spoke in low tones at first, but soon the dam broke. Under the vast sky, they laid everything bare. Dad admitted, with a heavy heart, that he had been too rigid and too demanding. Mom, her voice trembling, confessed that she had been too absorbed in her own world, neglecting Myra's needs. Myra, tears in her eyes, whispered that she had let her anger get the best of her, pushing everyone away.

Coco, their loyal companion, had been by their side through everything, a silent witness to their joys and sorrows. But on that fateful journey, his strength began to fade. The lively bark that once echoed through their home grew faint, barely a whisper of what it had been. As they rushed to the nearest hospital, desperation and hope mingled with every breath they took. But it wasn't enough. In those final moments, Coco, their faithful friend, quietly slipped away, leaving behind a void far greater than any of the wounds they had been struggling to mend. The loss was profound, a heartache that felt impossible to soothe, as the presence that had once brought them so much comfort was gone forever.

Myra was shattered, her heartache spilling over in endless tears. The family, already struggling, found themselves lost in a sea of grief. The loss of Coco was too fresh, too raw, and the house felt emptier than ever before. And then, as if the Universe wasn't done testing their strength, the phone rang. The sound cut through the heavy silence like a knife. It was a call from India, a call they had never expected, nor were they prepared for. Myra's grandfather, the gentle soul who had always been a pillar of wisdom and warmth, had passed away.

The news hit them like a tidal wave, pulling them under once more. The family huddled together, clinging to each other as the weight of yet another tragedy pressed down on them. Their tears flowed freely, their hearts breaking anew. It seemed as though the world had conspired to pile one heartache after another upon them. They couldn't help but wonder, in their darkest moments, if there would ever be an end to the sorrow that had engulfed their lives. They decided to go to India immediately.

Myra had always been close to her grandpa, who constantly encouraged her to follow her dreams. His loss hit them all hard, casting a shadow over their visit. India didn't feel the same this time.

However, being in India surrounded by a large extended family – grandparents, uncles, aunts, cousins, and even second cousins – who all loved and adored her, seemed to calm her tremendously. They were captivated by everything about her, from the way she talked and walked, to how she danced and played her guitar. They made time for her, taking her out, sitting together to play cards, watching movies, or visiting restaurants.

Slowly, Myra found her stress beginning to melt away. Without the pressures of peers or studies, she enjoyed bonding with her relatives and friends. She even performed for them and, in doing so, felt a sense of renewal. By the time it was time to go back, Myra felt hopeful about life once again.

Her parents, sensing the emotional toll everything had taken on Myra, believed she could benefit from counselling. Upon their return, she sat down for a session, pouring out her heart to the counsellor, recounting all that had transpired.

The counsellor listened patiently, then gently guided Myra to see things from a new perspective. "You've been through a lot," the counsellor said, "but remember, your values should always come first. Friends will follow. Just be yourself—kind and true to who you are— and the right people will naturally gravitate towards you. And don't forget, your studies are important too. They're the foundation for your future."

Myra left the session with a lighter heart and a clearer mind, ready to find balance in her life once more.

Her father enrolled her in special coaching classes for maths and other subjects, hoping it would set her on the path to recovery. They worked diligently to prepare her for the SAT [23] exam. At first, her progress was slow, but gradually, her grades began to improve. Every time someone else topped the class, she would cry, feeling the sting of knowing she was capable of more. But as she focused more on her studies, the academic challenges started to ease the burden of her loneliness, slowly but surely helping her regain her confidence.

Myra's life brightened when she became friends with Tina, her spirited Gujarati neighbour from school. Tina, with her vibrant red hair and distinctive nose ring, brought a burst of colour and energy into Myra's world. Their friendship blossomed effortlessly, and soon, sleepovers became a cherished routine, each night overflowing with laughter and shared secrets.

As their bond grew stronger, Myra's parents, who had initially been cautious, began to warm up to Tina's influence. They finally gave their approval, and Myra embraced the transformation with enthusiasm. She dyed her hair a shimmering golden hue, her eyes sparkling with excitement, as she adorned herself with a delicate nose and ear piercing.

With newfound confidence, Myra shifted her diet, trading in cheesy indulgences for crisp salads and fresh veggies. The change was almost magical; her skin began to clear, and her once-frequent pimples faded away. The pièce de résistance came when her mother, sensing her daughter's joy and growth, gifted her a complete makeup set. Myra's heart leapt with surprise and gratitude, the set shimmering like a promise of new beginnings.

---

23 *SAT: Scholastic Assessment Test*

After months of relentless effort, she finally cracked the SAT exam. Her score, though decent, fell short of her expectations, leaving her deeply disheartened. Sensing her despair, her father offered words of encouragement. "You've worked so hard, Myra, now it's time to move forward and apply to good colleges."

Determined to support her, her dad took on the role of mentor, guiding her through the college application process. As she sat at her desk, preparing to write the essential essay for her university applications, a storm of emotions swirled within her. She opened her laptop, feeling the weight of her experiences pressing down on her.

In that moment of reflection, she began to type, pouring out her feelings onto the screen. The title she chose seemed to capture everything she had endured: "Me and My Loneliness." As her fingers danced across the keyboard, her story unfolded – a poignant narrative of struggle, growth, and the quiet strength she had discovered within herself.

The family decided to undertake a journey across the country, a whirlwind tour of prestigious universities that spanned from New Jersey to Massachusetts. First, they wandered through the ivy-clad buildings of Princeton University, each step echoing with the whispers of centuries of academic excellence. In Pennsylvania, they marvelled at the innovative spirit of Carnegie Mellon University, where the air seemed charged with creative energy. Illinois held its own enchantment with the University of Chicago, its grand architecture and storied history inspiring awe. Finally, they arrived in Massachusetts, where Harvard University stood as a majestic beacon of academic tradition.

As Myra roamed these hallowed halls, her initial excitement began to transform into a profound realisation. The enormity of it all struck her like a tidal wave. The grandeur of these institutions, the legacy of the great minds who had walked their corridors, made her feel small and insignificant. Her heart raced with anxiety. Could she, a humble dreamer, truly belong in these exalted spaces? The thought of walking in the footsteps of those who had shaped the world before her filled her with both wonder and trepidation.

Fall in Pennsylvania was a sight to behold. The golden hues of sunrise kissed the mountains, while crimson maple trees swayed gently in the breeze, and crunchy leaves formed a vibrant carpet underfoot.With the acceptance letter from Carnegie Mellon University in her hand, Myra stood at the threshold of a new chapter, her heart brimming with dreams and hope. The weight of her bags seemed light compared to the immense promise of her future. As she prepared to step into the vibrant academic world ahead, she carried with her not just belongings but the culmination of a journey marked by struggle, growth, and unyielding determination. Myra was ready to embrace the extraordinary journey that awaited her.

Author Speak

Life is full of ups and downs, so do not lose hope while facing challenges, for it is through perseverance that you will find triumph. In today's world, young people are grappling with a loneliness that seems more pervasive than ever before. This is due to cell phones, those tiny screens that draw us in and pull us away from the real connections we crave. And it's not just the teenagers; even parents find themselves lost in a sea of work or their own digital distractions, leaving their children to navigate the turbulent waters of growing up alone.

But hear this: you are not powerless. Take charge of your life and make a conscious effort to forge genuine connections. Do not merely drift through your days, but actively seek out friendships that are rooted in mutual respect, kindness, and love. These are the bonds that will endure, the relationships that will sustain you through life's challenges.

Be vigilant about the company you keep, for the wrong influences can lead you astray, down paths fraught with danger and regret. Instead, devote your energy to pursuits that ignite your passions. Set goals that challenge you and hobbies that bring you joy. In doing so, you will find yourself surrounded by others who share your interests, and, in those shared passions, true friendships will blossom.

And remember, do not neglect your studies. Education is not just a duty, but a foundation upon which your future will be built. Balance your life with care, giving time to both learning and to the friendships that nourish your spirit.

10

ECHOES OF A LOST SON

A life squandered in the pursuit of escape is a life lost to the abyss!

Bhanumathi, and Narayan, were a distinguished couple residing in the quaint town of Pedana, nestled in the heart of Andhra Pradesh. Their lives were marked by prosperity and comfort. They owned a grand function hall that hosted various local events and celebrations, while their extensive farmlands provided a steady source of income through rents. The couple's affluence and stability offered them a secure and fulfilling lifestyle.

Their only son, Phani Kumar, was an ambitious eighteen year old with a singular dream: to become a doctor. His parents were thrilled by his aspirations, hoping to see him fulfil this noble ambition. However, Phani Kumar faced a significant hurdle. He was unable to pass the highly competitive entrance exam required for medical schools in India, which cast a shadow of uncertainty over his future.

Phani Kumar began exploring alternative paths to secure a seat in a Medical College. He discovered a promising opportunity when he learnt that he could gain admission to Medical Schools in Russia, which offered high-quality programmes at relatively affordable tuition fees. After considering various options, he decided to apply to Kazan Federal University, an esteemed institution located in Kazan. This vibrant city, situated east of Moscow, was one of Russia's leading cities, making it an ideal destination for his Medical Studies.

Excited by this chance, Phani Kumar prepared for his journey. His parents, were elated by the prospect of their son pursuing his dreams abroad. They supported him wholeheartedly, ensuring that he had everything he needed for this new chapter of his life. As Phani embarked on his journey to Russia, his parents continued to provide financial support, sending money regularly to cover his living expenses and educational costs.

During his four years of medical education in Kazan, Phani Kumar maintained a close connection with his family. He visited them once a year during the summer vacation, cherishing these reunions as precious moments of family bonding. The distance and time apart were challenging, but the shared joy of these visits helped bridge the gap.

One day, Phani Kumar made a long-awaited call to his parents, his voice brimming with something they couldn't quite place. "I'm coming back to India for good," he announced, leaving them breathless with pride and anticipation. They could hardly wait to have their son back home, to see for themselves how far he had come in chasing his dreams.

"Is your course over?" they asked eagerly.

His reply, however, caught them off guard. "No," he said. "I don't like it here. I'm coming back, but I'm not alone. My friend, Lubna, is coming with me. She'll be staying with us for a while, so please prepare a room for her."

His words hung in the air, heavy and unfamiliar. His parents were aghast, struggling to process what they had just heard. They couldn't help but feel as if the son they once knew had become a stranger. What had happened to the young man who left with such clear goals? What had become of him?

Phani, a tall, lanky young man returned home with a strikingly beautiful Russian woman – tall, blonde, with piercing blue eyes that seemed to hold a world of mystery. She looked like a living doll, delicate yet commanding, and her presence filled the room with a strange tension. Phani's parents greeted them awkwardly, their smiles thin with uncertainty, as they tried to mask the confusion swirling in their minds. Who was this woman? And what was her relationship with their son?

It didn't take long for the truth to surface. Phani and Lubna were more than just friends; they were in a relationship. The realisation hit his parents like a wave, unsettling and unexpected. Soon after, Phani began asking them for money more frequently. He and Lubna took trips together, travelling to Agra to see the Taj Mahal and then to the picturesque valleys of Kashmir. Upon their return, they settled into a routine that resembled that of a married couple, sharing a life under the same roof.

Phani and Lubna spoke to each other in Russian, a language that left his parents feeling even more isolated in their own home. The unfamiliar words, the intimate glances – they all added to the growing sense of unease. Phani's parents watched from a distance, struggling to grasp the changes in their son and the life he had chosen, feeling as if a barrier had been erected between them and the young man they had once known so well.

Eventually, unable to bear the growing tension any longer, Phani's parents decided to confront him. They needed answers, and the truth they uncovered was far more devastating than they had imagined. Phani confessed that he had failed to pass his exams and was, in fact, a university dropout. The image of their ambitious son crumbled before their eyes.

As the conversation continued, more dark revelations surfaced. Phani had been spending his days in bars where he had met Lubna. Far from the sophisticated woman they had imagined, she was a bar girl, abandoned and struggling to survive. Phani's parents were shocked, their hearts heavy with a mix of sorrow and disbelief.

But the worst was yet to come. They soon realised that Phani had fallen into a dangerous spiral. He was not just an alcoholic but also a drug addict. His behaviour had become erratic and violent, lashing out at both his parents and Lubna. The gentle, loving son they had raised was now a stranger, capable of extorting money from them with threats and intimidation. Their once peaceful home had turned into a place of fear and anxiety, where they lived in constant dread of Phani's next outburst. Even Lubna, who had once seemed so strong and independent, bore the brunt of his anger, enduring both physical and emotional abuse.

After enduring the tumultuous life with Phani for as long as she could, Lubna finally reached her breaking point. One evening, she quietly approached Phani's parents, her eyes filled with a mix of sorrow and resolve. She expressed her wish to return to Russia, to leave behind the chaos that had consumed her life. Sensing her desperation, Phani's parents, who had grown to care for her in their own way, didn't hesitate. They bought her a ticket, understanding that this was likely the only escape she had from their son's destructive behaviour.

On the day of her departure, they accompanied her to the airport. The atmosphere was heavy with unspoken words and emotions too complex to unravel. Just as they were about to say their final goodbyes, Lubna turned to them, her voice trembling. She confessed that she was pregnant. The words hung in the air like a weight too heavy to bear, leaving Phani's parents stunned and speechless. They exchanged a glance, the gravity of the situation sinking in.

Unsure of what to say or do, they offered her what little advice they could muster. "It's best for you to return to Russia," they urged gently, their voices tinged with worry. "Take care of yourself and the baby. It's the right decision."

With tears in her eyes, Lubna nodded, understanding that they were right. Moments later, she disappeared into the bustling airport, leaving Phani's parents standing alone, overwhelmed by the enormity of what had just transpired and uncertain of what the future would hold.

After Lubna's departure, Phani's anger only intensified. The house that once echoed with the sound of laughter now trembled under the force of his rage. One night, in a fit of uncontrollable fury, he slammed his fists into the television, shattering the screen into a spray of glass. His parents watched in horror, their bodies shaking with fear, as their son stood amidst the wreckage of what was once a peaceful home.

Desperate to save him, they made the painful decision to put him in a rehab centre, hoping it would be the first step towards reclaiming the son they had lost. But Phani, driven by his addictions, managed to escape and return home, more defiant than ever.

In a final attempt to help him, they offered him the chance to manage the family's function hall business. Perhaps the responsibility would anchor him, they thought, and give him a purpose. But their hopes were quickly dashed. Phani took advantage of the opportunity, siphoning off money to fuel his drinking and drug habits. The function hall, once a source of pride and livelihood, became just another casualty of Phani's downward spiral.

His parents, now frail and defeated, could only watch helplessly as Phani continued to destroy everything in his path, the weight of their helplessness growing heavier with each passing day.

In the quiet of their home, Narayan and Bhanumathi sat together, the weight of their despair pressing down on them like a heavy blanket. The room was dimly lit, casting long shadows across their faces, mirroring the sadness that had settled in their hearts.

Narayan broke the silence, his voice thick with regret. "I never bought you jewellery," he began, staring at his weathered hands. "I never took you around the world, like I always promised. Every penny we had, I saved for our son, thinking we were securing his future. And now, look at what he's become—a dacoit in our own home. He has ruined us, Bhanumathi."

She didn't say anything, just nodded, her eyes brimming with unshed tears. Narayan's heart ached seeing her so broken, and in that moment, he made a decision. The very next day, he bought her a diamond necklace, the one she had admired years ago but had never asked for. He also booked a twenty-day tour to Europe, something they had only ever dreamt about. When he told her, a small, sad smile tugged at her lips, but it was clear that neither of them could fully escape the sorrow that had taken root in their lives.

They informed Phani about their plans, hoping, perhaps, this trip would bring them some peace and some distance from the turmoil he had caused. Phani barely acknowledged them, lost in his own world of anger and addiction.

The following day, chaos erupted. Phani had gone to the function hall, as he often did when he needed money. But this time, the accountant refused to give him unaccounted cash. A heated argument ensued, voices rising, and fists clenched. Frustrated and furious, Phani stormed out, his rage propelling him to his bike.

Without a second thought, he sped into the night, the roar of the engine echoing his anger. The highway stretched out before him, dark and endless. He pushed the bike faster, the cool night air whipping past him, but his mind was a whirlwind of thoughts. He didn't see the lorry until it was too late. It hit him with full force, sending him and the bike crashing into the asphalt. The night swallowed the sound of the impact, and with it, Phani's life.

Narayan and Bhanumathi were left with a grief too deep to express, their dreams of a peaceful future shattered. The diamond necklace, still in its velvet box, sat untouched on the dresser, and the tickets to Europe lay forgotten. All that remained was the crushing sorrow of losing their son and the haunting emptiness of a future that could never be mended.

Author Speak

Many young people are unaware that the drug trade is part of a global conspiracy. Nearby, the Golden Crescent, stretching across Afghanistan, Iran, and Pakistan, and the Golden Triangle, encompassing Burma, Laos, and Thailand, are major sources of heroin and other illicit drugs. These substances are funnelled into India by terrorists and hostile forces intent on destabilising and corrupting the nation's youth. The devastating effects are particularly stark along India's North-Western and North-Eastern borders.

To the youth, I urge you to cherish and protect your lives. Embrace the beauty of life and resist the lure of this dangerous path. Life is a precious gift, a boon that deserves to be lived fully and meaningfully. Let us honour it by making wise choices and forging a future free from the shadows of addiction.

11

DRUG BUST

Say no to peer pressure! Say no to drugs!

The Government office of Excise and Prohibition was bustling with activity as the news of the appointment of a new Director - Akun Sabharwal IPS [24]spread like wildfire. The young Sub-Inspectors had spurred to action, preparing to receive their boss-to-be.

Akun had secured the 33rd rank in his first attempt in the U.P.S.C [25]exam and had opted for the Indian Police Service. There was more to him than his academic achievements; he was an avid cyclist, mountaineer, and marathoner. He had completed seven tough marathons across India, showcasing his endurance and determination. His passion for adventure sports was well-known, and it was no secret that he had the zest and energy to perform his new role effectively.

As the staff stood at attention, eagerly awaiting his first appearance at 10 am, dressed in his crisp khaki uniform, Akun walked into the

---

24 *I.P.S – Indian Police Service*
25 *U.P.S.C – Union Public Service Commission*

office. He was ushered into the meeting room where he met his team.

After the initial introductions, he started delegating their duties and responsibilities. The young officers were eager to learn, prove themselves, and serve their country to the best of their abilities. The office was full of promise, with a sense of camaraderie and team spirit building amongst them already.

Elsewhere, when the doorbell rang, Anika, a sixteen-year-old girl, rushed out of the house to find the courier delivery man with her long-awaited parcel. Her mother, who was sitting behind a computer screen, asked her what it was. "It's nothing much," Anika replied, "just some Cadbury chocolates."

Her mother warned her that it's not good to have too much sugar. Anika's father, who looked at his daughter with love and admiration, expressed his discomfort with online shopping and how everything in their lives happens so quickly in this technological era.

Anika took the parcel into her room and locked the door behind her. As she opened the package, she gazed at the innocent-looking brown Cadbury chocolate. However, what nobody knew was that it was laced with a forbidden substance. She quickly secured it in a box and hid it behind the clothes in her wardrobe.

Anika's parents held high positions in the corporate world; her mother was the HR[26] Director in Ozone Ltd, while her father was the CFO[27] in a leading hospital. Anika was their only daughter, and they had great expectations from her.

An urgent meeting was convened by the Excise and Prohibition office following the receipt of crucial intelligence regarding the sale of drugs at the city's most happening pubs. Akun formed a specialised task force

---

26   *HR - Human Resource*
27   *CFO - Chief Finance Officer*

comprised of young inspectors to track the traffickers and capture them red-handed in the act. He assigned the job to his most trusted officers, Vignesh and Asha.

The strategy was that these sleuths would disguise themselves as ordinary pub patrons and frequent the pubs on weekends, posing as enthusiastic party-goers, to gain the trust of the dealers.

Anika checked her phone. There was a message from the secret group. This Friday, they were asked to visit "Brownies and Weasels," a new pub, for supplies. She went home to plan out this rendezvous.

Anika told her mother, "Ma, there is a party at 'Brownies and Weasels' this Friday hosted by a few of my classmates. I really want to go to..."

Her mother responded, "Sorry, Anika, we cannot allow you to go. You are too young for parties like this."

Anika then asked heatedly, "But why? I am not a child anymore. I am sixteen and capable of making my own decisions."

Her father tried to calm her and said, "We understand that you are growing up, but we have to ensure your safety and well-being first."

Anika, cajoling them, said, "I will be safe, I promise. And you can even see me on a video call while I am there. You don't have to worry then."

Mother was still hesitant and said, "Anika, we are not comfortable with you going to a night party at this age."

Anika retorted in a loud voice, "I can't socialise with friends and have fun. I'll have no friends if it's like this! I am embarrassed that you are so backward in your thoughts."

Her mother sternly said, "That was so rude! Is this the way to speak to your parents?"

Anika, unfazed, continued, "Then why did you put me in an international school? So that I could be a recluse and never socialise with anyone?" She said with sarcasm.

Her mother told her, "We put you in an international school because we want you to have good education and a bright future."

Anika didn't stop there and said angrily, "But what's the point of a bright future if I can't enjoy my life and have fun with my friends?"

Anika was shaking with emotion and burst into tears as a last resort.

Her mother was disturbed by this behaviour, and her father tried to do some damage control.

He said, "Calm down, dear. We understand your point of view, but we also want you to understand ours. Let's talk about this and come to a compromise."

Anika screamed, "I don't want a compromise. I want to go to the party."

Her mother relented and said, "Alright, Anika. We trust you to make the right decisions and be responsible. You may go, come back on time."

Both her parents were exasperated and worried.

Undercover sleuths Vignesh and Asha of the task force had been visiting the pub "Brownies and Weasels" regularly, asking for more than just a drink and a puff. After nearly a month, a man named Rafael approached Asha and discreetly offered to supply a range of banned drugs on the condition of confidentiality. She agreed. He added her to a WhatsApp group. Slowly, she introduced Vignesh to Rafael, introducing him as her friend.

Asha's cell phone beeped, 'maal' will be delivered on Friday night at "Brownies and Weasels". She sprang into action. Director Akun was informed. A trap was laid.

It was Friday night. Both Vignesh and Asha reached "Brownies and Weasels" at 11 pm. The pub was filled with blaring music as young kids danced and enjoyed themselves. The DJ provided a continuous stream of loud beats, energising the atmosphere.

Asha and Vignesh navigated through the crowded space, scanning the room as they walked in. They noticed Rafael standing near the toilet as expected. Anika was also at the pub attending her school party. She noticed Rafael too and approached him. They exchanged a few words, and Rafael pulled out a small packet of candies from his pocket, offering them to Anika. She hesitated for a moment but then grabbed them all and stuffed them into her purse.

Asha observed the interaction between Anika and Rafael. She discreetly signalled Rafael to step outside. He understood. Asha and Rafael stepped out of the pub into the relatively quieter outdoors. They found a secluded spot from prying eyes.

Asha took out a wad of cash from her pocket and handed it over to Rafael, who gave her a small packet in return. They quickly completed the exchange, trying to remain inconspicuous.

Suddenly, Vignesh, who followed them outside unnoticed, stepped forward and overpowered Rafael. He swiftly confiscated Rafael's phone, leaving him stunned and unable to react.

"You're under arrest for illegal activities. We have evidence against you," stated Vignesh in an authoritative tone.

Rafael's face contorted with shock and fear as he realised the gravity of the situation. The music from the pub continued to blare in the background, contrasting the tension of the moment outside.

Director Akun stood by the window in his office room, looking out at a schoolyard filled with bustling children and their vibrant uniforms. However, there was an underlying sense of distress in his mind.

"How can school children be taking drugs? This is alarming!" he murmured to himself.

There was disbelief written all over his face as he contemplated the matter. His heart was burdened, knowing that the youth was falling prey to harmful habits.

"What will happen to the future of our country?" he whispered to himself.

He turned away from the window, walked back to his desk, and rang the buzzer.

Vignesh came in, holding a stack of files in his hands.

Akun briskly and firmly instructed him, "I want all the kids listed on his WhatsApp group to come for counselling, along with their parents. We need to address this issue immediately."

Vignesh promptly said, "Sir, they've arrived. They are all waiting outside."

Akun nodded as his eyes focused on the files.

Without looking up, Akun said, "Send them in one by one."

Vignesh opened the office door, and Anika, accompanied by her worried parents, walked in. Anika's face was pale and full of fear. Her parents' faces were shocked and ashen.

Akun gently asked them to take their seats.

Looking directly at Anika, he asked her, "Do you know that consuming drugs is a serious offence? If you are found sharing it with someone, you can be booked for drug peddling. Your punishment can be imprisonment for 6 months to 20 years. Your life will be ruined in either case," he said in a firm voice and continued, "However, we are here to help you overcome this challenge. You will have to attend a mandatory counselling session, and no charges shall be pressed on you," he added.

Looking at her parents, he counselled them that they must take time off work and pay more attention to their kids. "You may go now," he concluded the meeting.

On reaching home, Anika burst into tears and sobbed uncontrollably.

"I am sorry, Ma and Pa. I did not realise the seriousness of what I was doing. Forgive me," she sobbed.

Her mother gently but firmly asked her, "Do you want to become a drug peddler like Rafael and destroy many lives, or become a great human being like Officer Akun Sabharwal and save lives?"

Anika assured them with a change of heart, "I want to become an IPS officer like Akun Sir. I will study well and do my best to be of use to society at large. I will make you proud one day." Her parents hugged her as she continued to cry tears of regret.

Author Speak

Teenage years should be dedicated to pursuing your dreams and discovering who you are, not falling into the trap of peer pressure, bad habits, and addictions. Be mindful of the friends you choose and focus on hobbies that genuinely interest you. You are a bundle of energy, find productive ways to channelise it and stay away from drugs.

12

BOUGAINVILLEA BLOOMS

The Universe shall conspire to make our dreams come true!

At sunrise in Pleasant Valley, a beautiful peacock glided gracefully atop a boulder, perched itself on it, and cawed, heralding the daybreak. Several birds chirped in concurrence. I stepped out of my house for a morning walk. As I walked downhill, I encountered a bunch of peahens strolling, crossing the "Desier-Crest," a recently restored lake. Moving past the lake, I started walking uphill.

With satisfaction, I observed that subsequent rounds of tree planting campaigns by the community had covered the roadsides and slopes with Forest Flame, Ashoka, Neem, Sal, and other fruit-bearing trees. Admiring the unique boulder formation along my way up, I got out of breath as I reached the top. The serene twin lakes instantly calmed my nerves as I sat down to meditate.

Feeling refreshed, I walked along the ramp, which separated the lakes and reached the viewpoint. The orange sky filled my heart with warmth. The skyscrapers stood like proud sentinels, announcing the arrival of a new age, while the tombs in the far end harked back to the old times. The confluence of the old and new seemed to melt here. Looking below, I saw the splendid row houses. Each villa had a small garden in front, a couple of cars parked, and from atop they looked like toy homes. I located our house, which was the second one from the right. A deep, narrow gorge with steep sides defined the space between the viewpoint and where I lived.

'How would it be if myriad coloured bougainvillea[28] creepers hung from the edge of the path opposite our home into the gorge?' I questioned myself. 'They would look stunning from here,' I thought. Excited with the idea and full of enthusiasm, I ran downhill nonstop till I reached my abode. The very next day, I went to the nursery and bought all the available colours of bougainvillea and planted them along the edge of the path opposite our home.

Each day, I watered the plants, occasionally loosened the soil, sprinkled manure, and cared for them. Six months had passed, then slowly a year passed by, yet they continued to be small shrubs. Each day, as I drove to my office, I noticed a couple of tall, well-grown bougainvillea shrubs along the roadside. A bright cherry-red one and a splash of white. They looked stunning, imposing, and so colourful. I admired them and felt sad for the ones I had planted. Sometimes, wild flowers bloom and flourish, while carefully planted and tended plants do not.

Five years had passed by. My plants had not yet grown . I was disappointed and called for professional help to seek advice on what must be done so that they bloom.

Subramaniam, a very senior gardener, inspected the plants and explained to me that these plants needed bright sunlight. He pointed out that they were growing under the shade of Sal trees. Only after he stated it, I noticed that the gorge below was full of Sal trees, and

---

28 *An ornamental, shrubby climbing plant that is widely cultivated in the tropics. The insignificant flowers are surrounded by large, brightly coloured papery bracts, which persist on the plant for a long time.*

yes, my bougainvillea was in the shade. 'You should have planted these in your garden where there is ample sunlight,' he remarked. I nodded as I realised the problem, but nothing could be done now. My poor bougainvilleas!

In the month of February, the Sal trees started shedding leaves. The weather became warm and windy. At nights, one could hear the wind whisper in the valley. Because of the gorge, sometimes the sound of the wind would be so loud that you would feel as if the spirits in the valley were talking to each other. February turned to March, and the weather became hot and dusty; the season of pollen exchange had arrived.

It so happened that a lady who lived at the end of the slope in the valley developed a serious allergy to the pollen of Sal trees. Her eyes turned red and watered all the time. She had a runny nose, her head felt heavy, and she frequently sneezed. Neither Allopathy, Ayurveda, or Homeopathy medicines could alleviate her discomfort.

Unable to watch her suffer, her loving and empathetic husband appealed to the Valley Committee to get rid of the Sal trees. He impressed upon them how harmful the Sal pollen was and proposed that planting Neem trees in its place would be salubrious. The committee called for an emergency meeting regarding the issue. They discussed all the aspects of the problem at hand. Though it was an expensive proposition, they agreed to it.

The labour force descended into the valley and swiftly chopped off all the Sal trees. The valley looked barren and dry, devoid of the green. Come April, and the sun blazed. Days were long, and nights were short. The bright rays of the sun seemed unrelenting and scorched the boulders in the valley. They, in turn, reflected and radiated the heat around.

With the shadow of the Sal trees gone, my bougainvillea slowly picked up growth. The effulgence of the sun was right upon them; they started growing swiftly in a few days. Their spectacularly coloured papery bracts bloomed to my pleasure. The beautiful colours of pink, purple, red, yellow, orange, and white made a rainbow outside my house. The bushy creepers descended slowly onto the valley, just as I had wanted them to. I saw hummingbirds and butterflies hovering over them, to my delight. At last, my bougainvillea bloomed!

Author Speak

There is profound meaning in this small anecdote. Sometimes, even though we try our best, results are not delivered. Sometimes it all seems hopeless, yet we must keep going on without losing hope. The Universe will conspire to remove the obstacles in our path and make our dreams come true. Believe in God, yourself, and your dream...

13

FROM RUSH HOUR TO SOLITUDE

Mother Nature always nourishes us!

As I looked out of the window of the study, my gaze got fixed on the plants outside. The proud Christmas tree stood like a sentinel with its spiky arms. Hibiscus flowers of all hues had bloomed and speckled the green cover. An assortment of crotons and roses adorned the steps leading to my door. On the far end, a bunch of hummingbirds had gathered and were chatting incessantly. Good monsoon had blessed my gardening efforts!

A large brown cat with green eyes walked up to my window and stared at me. She did not seem frightened. I got up from my chair and went out. "Meeeow," she cried. I ignored her and went about plucking flowers. She was insistent and followed me around. I realised she was hungry and went inside to get her some milk. She purred in happiness and drank it. Never before had I had time to notice the friends' nature had provided for me.

Thud! I heard a dull sound from my balcony. As I rushed there to see what it was, I saw that a nest had fallen from the fan mounted on the wall. Two baby pigeons were on the floor, along with the twigs, sticks, and dead leaves scattered about. My heart skipped a beat. I bent down and checked for damages. Thankfully, there were none. The newborns were cosily curled up next to each other with their eyes shut. I brought a hanging wooden pot from inside, put small cushions inside it to fill it up, then transferred the remains of the nest and the babies into it, and hung it on the same fan. Was it telepathy or a mother's sixth sense? I noticed the mother pigeon circling my balcony. A warm feeling welled in my heart as I smiled with satisfaction that her babies were safe.

It was time to take 'Don and Hazel', our pet German shepherds, for a walk. My son helped me in this difficult task; both of us held them on the leash and walked them to the shooting range in the battalion grounds. I couldn't help admiring them for their courage, loyalty, and their instincts to guard. Both of them wagged their tails in excitement and licked my hand every now and then to show love and gratitude. Felt so rich with it.

I would seldom pause to admire nature or spend lazy afternoons with birds, cats, and dogs. I never had time for yoga, meditation, or leisure nature walks. Life seemed such a rush; where did all the time go? Thanks to this pandemic, today, after four months of staying at home, cooking, washing dishes, mopping, sweeping, making beds, and dusting, I have changed from a restless traveller, socialite, teacher, and researcher to a homemaker, gardener, nature lover, and much more. It's been a time of spiritual reckoning. I am at peace with myself and love this solitude.

Author Speak

I will share some statistics which will speak for themselves;

In the year 1920, the human population was 1.8 billion, wild tigers numbered one lakh, and forest cover was 5 billion hectares in the world. But, in the year 2024, the human population has reached 8 billion, tigers are 5574, and forest cover is down by 20%, only 4.06 billion hectares.

We have been overexploiting nature. We produce millions of pounds of trash every day and dump it in landfills. Tons of sewage, industrial, and agricultural wastes are thrown into the rivers each day. A fresh water crisis is looming large.

Our growing population is destroying wildlife habitat. Thirty thousand species go extinct each year. Overfishing is leading to an imbalance in ocean life.

Our ozone layer is damaged, exposing us to harmful UVB radiation. The air we breathe is polluted and unfit for human living conditions, as per WHO.

The Arctic glaciers are melting, sea levels are rising. global warming and climate change are serious threats to our existence.

Alas! This is the planet Earth we have inherited.

Hence, it is vital to contribute to the improvement of the environment.

In our individual capacity, we can plant trees, gift saplings, and dispose of trash appropriately by segregating dry and wet trash. We can build our own vegetable waste compost pit. We can reuse, recycle, and reduce at home. We can switch off lights and fans when not in use, ensure taps are turned off after use. We can reduce paper usage and resort to e-reading, and also use clay Ganesh during festival time. These are a few ways we can revive nature. The list is endless...